HELLO, GOODBYE

Stories, Essays and Poems
For the 21st Century

Selected and edited by
Gay Baines and Mary Ann Eichelberger

July Literary Press ❖ Buffalo, NY ❖ 2004
www.julyliterarypress.com

Acknowledgments

Grateful acknowledgment is made to the following publications where certain of the contents originally appeared, or will appear, as noted: *The Asheville Poetry Review* ("A Night of Yelling Couldn't Coax Cows out of Deadly Barn"); Palanquin Poetry Series ("The Woman's Field Guide to Survival"); *North American Review* ("A Poem Speaks to the Poet" under different title); *Ibis Review* ("Memory"); *Blue Mesa Review* ("Cinderella Verité"); *Words of Wisdom* and *Nagoya Writes* ("Fingers of Coincidence"); *Serving Suggestion* ("reserved for senses"); *The Buffalo News* ("Hosing Down Cows"); *muse-apprentice-guild website* ("Snow in Leningrad"); *Rattle 15: Poetry for the 21st Century* ("The Largeness of Flowers"); *What Language*, Slipstream, Niagara Falls, NY, 2002 ("Pulling Poe Out of Baltimore"); *Practical Gods*, Penguin, New York, NY, 2001 ("Numbers" and "The Lace Maker," also previously published in *Salmagundi*); Davoren Hanna Poetry Competition 2002 ("All Day I Have Been Afraid"—3rd Place winner); *California Quarterly* ("Offerings"); *Family Times* ("Moms and Bads"); *East Aurora Advertiser* ("Bringing Home the Bacon"); *No One Is the Same Again*, Quarterly Review of Literature, 1999 ("Some Nights the Dark Hill" and "Night Piece"); *Eureka Literary Magazine* ("Placards"); *Eclipse* ("Things You Do"); *Playboy* (Tuba City); *Inkwell* and *Sender* ("The Two Alices"); *Poet's Paper* ("Whose Refugees?"); *Ibbetson Street Press* (Harvard Square on Christmas Eve)

Cover painting by Clare Poth
Editorial assistant: Barbara Maynor
Legal consultant: Paul Poth
Website designed by Thomas Maynor

Copyright 2004 by July Literary Press

Orffeo Printing Co., Inc. ❖ 4490 Broadway ❖ Depew, NY 14043

Table of Contents

PART 1

PART 2

PART 3

PART 3

PART 4

Part 1

taste summer
licked from the lips of a swimmer

One Great Poem

I want to write one great poem
that will win one of the contests
in Poets & Writers Magazine.
They will put in a little photograph
of me, half smiling or not smiling.
(A photographer once told me that I
looked better when I did not smile).
The magazine will write little things
about me being a promising writer
even though I am forty-five
and the promises
have already been kept.
I want to write just one great poem
that college students will either get
or not get or hate or puzzle over
and write papers about with thesis
sentences and all that and misread
and read right to help them be wise.
I want high school valedictorians
to recite it at commencements.
Everyone will nod and say,
"Yes, yes it is so true, so true."
But they will not really be sure
they know exactly
what is true about it.
But it will sound true and they
will sense that it is true and wise.
That will be enough.
I will be asked to speak at small
colleges in Indiana
and upstate New York.
I will look for profound
things to say and read my
one great poem
and it will be enough.

– Dan Sklar

Numbers

Two hands may not always be better than one,
But four feet and more are likely to prove
More steady than two as we wade a stream
Holding above our heads the ark
Of our covenant with the true and beautiful,
A crowd of outlaw pagans hot on our heels,
The shades of our ancestors cheering us on.

Three friends with poems at Mac's this evening
Are closer than one to the truth if we lift our glasses
To the poet that Mac proposes
We toast before beginning, Li Po.

Three votes that the poem I've brought is finished
Versus one turn of the head too slight
For anyone not on the watch to notice
As Li Po demurs.

Is this America, land of one man, one vote,
I want to ask, or the China of one-man rule,
Of emperors who believe they're gods?

Li Po, now only a thin layer of dust
In Szechwan Province though somehow
Still standing inches behind his words.

Five of my lines, he suggests with a nod,
Out of the score I've written,
Are fine as they are if I provide them
The context that they deserve and speak them
Without misgivings and with greater gusto.

Five lead out from the kitchen
Past a dozen detours to a single bridge
That must be crossed in order to reach a homeland
Eager for my arrival.

This is the message I get from a prophet whose signs
Are a threadbare coat and an empty cupboard,
Proof he's never written for anyone but himself
And the dead teachers easy to count
On the stiff fingers of one hand.

In memory of Mac Hammond

– Carl Dennis

Passion Fruit

I slow my spoon, wanting
every green and yellow slurp
around each soft-eyed seed,
thick syrup more delicious than
sun-warmed summer peaches.

Then I remember papaya, mango,
cherries, their strumpet luster,
the sweet musk of dusk-pink guavas,
oranges—golden juice, piquant rinds—
blackberries, raspberries,
my juice-stained fingers
inching through their vines,
and just-picked apples, tart,
crisp and dripping when I bit,

each a gift of pollen,
wind, insect, bird, centuries,
oceans crossed, and geologic drift.
Such succulence—
Earth's ardor
on my tongue.

– Rema Boscov

After Edward Hopper's Lighthouse Hill

...her presence was essential to his work
Edward Lucie-Smith

At first,
a simple scene—
a lighthouse,
an old gabled cottage
half in shadow,
grassy fields like ocean swells,
the sharp light
of a late summer afternoon.

But then—
that tall stiff whiteness
high above those mounds
of ochre grass.
That line of red in shadow.
That thin stream of cloud,
arrow-shaped—
a stain
on the darkening sky.

As Jo's presence
sweeps across
this lonely hill,
I want to know
what you were feeling
when you swirled your brush
in those blues and browns,
that white and red.

– Patricia Brodie

The Lace Maker

Holding the bobbins taut as she moves the pins,
She leans in close, inches away from the fabric
Fretted and framed on the wooden work board.

A young woman in a yellow dress
Whose lighter hair, bound tight to her head
But flowing about one shoulder,

Suggests the self-forgetful beauty of service,
Service to a discipline. Just so the painting
Forgets the background to focus on her.

Here she is, so close to the surface
The painter could touch her if he stretched his hand.
Close work in sympathy with close work.

The sewing cushion holding the colored threads
Suggests a painter's palette. So Vermeer
Offers a silent tribute to another artist

Who's increasing the number of beautiful
Useless things available in a world
That would be darker and smaller without them.

This is no time to ask if the woman
Wishes she were rich enough to buy the likeness,
If Vermeer can afford the lace she's making;

No time to consider them bandying compliments.
They work in silence, and you may look on
Only if you quiet your thoughts enough

To hear the click of her needles as you lean in close
(But not so close that you cast a shadow)
And the light touch of his brush on canvas.

– Carl Dennis

These Days

How often come
moments of grace
in the late, hard years.
It all turns luminous
as the moment in the sun
when the ant crawls by
bearing his crumb burden
of the time of the sifting
of the delicate flour grains
into the blue bowl.
It is a trick of seeing,
after all.

– Sally A. Fiedler

"Black Place 1944" by Georgia O'Keeffe

1
Hooded monks march
heads bent
eyes closed
they see only inner light
not the sun ahead

2
Somewhere beyond the rim
a desert of hot sand
flat reflections of the daystar
then light and flatness fall away
and with each fold
darkness grows
until an eye of black
penetrates backwards
tunnels beneath to
the soul of the desert
discovers the secret of cactus flowers
find the place where mirages grow

3
There is a valley
into which all color flows
greens and yellows
grays and browns
tumble into the ravine
gravity being the law
whereby color lives
and the gray snake
slithers down the river
hungry for
tint and hue.

– *V. Jane Schneeloch*

in rue 23.

bleached moon face
paces shore as a japanese
print is stamped across his mind
while he moves thru autumn sunrise.
he sways toward dinghy
tied to mossy ledge,
& scoops at red goldfish,
only to view, in his mind again,
an abstract piece by hans hoffman.
he had watered his book
on the terrace;
seeds were sprouting from its pages.
his mud book is a good book.
each word will become
a leaf & a paragraph.
with enuf thought, will bloom.

– *Guy R. Beining*

Joseph Scott Kierland

Tuba City

The road into the Navajo Nation runs circular through harsh open range. I'd been headed that way for hours, past clusters of mobile homes and modest ranch houses dotting the wide, stark landscape of chapparal and tumbleweed.

New signs of the modern world slowly popped into view like rising bubbles. A McDonald's appeared, and then a Taco Bell, and I could see a Wells Fargo Bank tucked in among the large mounds of earth that stood like secluded sentinels on either side of the two lane blacktop. A hand-painted sign appeared advertising DINOSAUR TRACKS. It leaned precariously against the burned out shell of an old Ford pickup. Further on a smaller sign read, "GO WARRIORS," and then finally a highway sign came into view saying Tuba City. A pale horse hung his head solemnly over an old wooden fence and stared out at me as I slowed down to let a pickup truck, filled with firewood, make a wide turn on a dirt road. The horse's eyes stayed with me as I passed and his steady gaze made me feel like an intruder that hadn't earned the right to see these simple things.

Usually these side trips ended with little accomplished except having done a favor for an old friend. The old friend in this case happened to be a man named Teddy Nighthorse whom I'd met in Tucson years ago. I always associated Teddy with spring training and our love for baseball. We'd gotten into the habit of meeting in Tucson at the end of a long winter and making the rounds together. We'd usually run into each other at one of the morning batting practices. We'd lean against the mesh fence and watch the warm-weather ritual of men stepping into a crudely marked box to try and smash a speeding ball with one inch of a round bat.

As a scout for the Arizona Diamondbacks my territory included southern California and an occasional trip up the coast to spy on the Giants. But there were months to go before spring training began so Teddy's sudden phone call surprised me. He'd asked me to come up and take a peek at a young pitcher, something he'd never done before, so I reluctantly agreed.

Looking at young prospects usually took place in the formal setting of a high school or college game. Baseball scouts showed up to study particular players in the faint hope that they'd be good enough to recruit. There'd be pages of statistics to go through before you arrived. Then you'd have to deal with the particular expectations of the young player and his coach. Isolated cases like Tuba City were less formal and usually you just encouraged the young player and then turned around and went home. So when I made the left on Moenave Street I had the feeling it would be just another turn around day.

I saw Teddy standing under the trees in the middle of the street. He waved me toward a dirt driveway and pointed to a parking place directly in front of a beatup dumpster. I began apologizing for being nearly an hour late but Teddy just smiled and said, "Did you bring the equipment?"

"Sure did," I said and opened the trunk to show him. The air had gotten colder, and the first thing I took out was my heavy leather jacket. A group of little Navajo boys surrounded us and stared into the trunk at my array of professional baseball equipment.

"This's just what we need," Teddy said as he picked up the catcher's equipment and opened a fresh box of baseballs. I reached in and grabbed one of the lighter bats and took my speed gun out of its leather case.

By the time I turned around Teddy had already started for the makeshift ball field behind us. I noticed how fit he looked for an older man. His straight white hair and leathery skin gave certain clues to his being somewhere in his sixties. Possibly early seventies. He moved slow and easy like an old cat and had probably been an athlete at one time. In all the years I'd known him we had never met outside the ballpark or talked about our past. I came out of the sandlots in the Bronx and Teddy had spent his life on an Indian reservation. That's all we knew about each other. We talked only about big league baseball and the approaching season. In fact, this was the first time I had ever ventured into what we both laughingly referred to as Teddy Country.

The group of nine-year-olds hung in close to us like a flock of colorful birds and helped Teddy carry the catcher's equipment to the broken-down backstop. On a signal from the old man one of the boys took off across Moenave Street and disappeared into a faded white building with a hand-painted sign over its front door that read First Presbyterian Church. I didn't know what the procedure would be but Teddy seemed to have everything under control.

"You did say the kid is left-handed...didn't you?" I asked while Teddy strapped on a chest protector and shin guards.

"Yeah, he's a southpaw and I'm waiting to see what he registers on that speed gun you brought," he said and punched the catcher's mitt.

I held out a shiny white baseball to see which dark-haired little kid would step up and throw the ball at him but they just giggled and backed away shyly.

"I sent one of the kids across the street to get him," Teddy said and I nodded as two of the boys picked up the box of baseballs and carried them out to the recently graded pitcher's mound. Teddy waddled over to the backstop to brush off homeplate and fill in the rain-rutted area around the batter's box with his cowboy boots. He seemed nervous and I could hear him telling the boys to stay out of the way.

I looked around at the few rows of stands, in need of paint, that ran the edge of the field along the baselines. I walked slowly across the infield and noticed a large patch of crab grass and weeds had been recently dug out and reseeded. I stepped around it, took out my measuring tape, and waved to one of the little boys to come over and hold the end of it at the top of the pitcher's mound while I slowly unravelled the sixty and a half feet to homeplate. I smiled over at Teddy still working on the batter's box and said, "This field may not look like much but it's got a perfect distance from the mound to homeplate."

"I didn't want the kid throwing the wrong distance so I measured and readjusted the whole thing," he said. "The height of the mound was a little trickier but I think we got that about right, too."

I rolled up the tape and glanced out at the school building behind the dumpsters. For the first time I noticed the windows were jammed with people. The left-handed kid had fans. The faces in the windows suddenly turned in unison to look at something through the leafless trees along Moenave Street, and I got a good look at the kid.

Large and lumbering and a bit overweight, he had a strong determination in his step as he headed directly for the backstop. His high cheekbones made his round face look even bigger, and a shock of black hair hung straight to his shoulders. He had on a bright red sweatshirt and blue jeans, and torn sneakers that were actually held together with pieces of string. Under his arm he carried an old, flat baseball glove that looked homemade and, as he went past the stands, he casually rubbed each boy's head for luck.

"This is Nick Costa. The man I told you about," Teddy said. When the kid extended his hand I could hardly grasp it all in mine. His handshake was gentle, almost weak, but his smile was big and strong. "This is Harold Bromley, the kid I wanted you to look at," Teddy said proudly from behind the catcher's mask.

"Everyone around here just calls me Shoe," the kid said.

"That's short for Big Shoe," Teddy added.

"Shoe. That's just fine."

"I've already warmed up," he said.

"Great. Let's get started," I said and Teddy squatted down behind homeplate.

"How old are you?" I asked the kid as we walked out to the mound.

"Almost eighteen," he answered softly and bent over to take one of the new baseballs out of the box. I watched his every move to see if he had any kind of an injury or handicap, or might be physically compensating for anything, but he moved smoothly around the mound. He flipped the ball to the plate in an easy warm-up motion and when Teddy threw the ball back he caught it as if he'd been doing it his whole life. He threw in another pitch a little faster, and I watched his arm motion to see where he released the ball and where he ended up on the mound after the delivery.

"You gonna put the gun on my fast ball?" he said and smiled.

"Ever have that done before?"

"No," he said. "Should be fun."

I had never heard anyone refer to the speed gun as *fun* before. Usually you tried to hide the gun from a young kid or even a professional when their speed began to drop late in a game. Some of the big league ballparks had even begun to display the speed of each pitch on their scoreboards. That put more pressure on the pitcher and the batters. But this kid looked at the speed gun as *fun*. I liked his attitude.

It felt like a storm rolling in and I glanced up at the school building. The lights had been turned on making it easier to see the people watching us from the windows.

"Whenever you're ready just let me know," I said and pulled up the collar on my leather jacket.

"Guess I'm ready," the big kid said.

"Just relax and give me a straight fast ball."

"Want me to try an' hit the corner?" he said.

"Why not?" I said and set the speed gun.

The kid nodded at Teddy crouched behind the plate, and he gave him a target on the inside corner for a left-handed batter. The kid went into a short windup and came down hard off the mound. His arm came across his body like a whip, and I heard him grunt as he released the ball. It slammed into the catcher's mitt. When I looked down the gun read ninety-eight miles an hour. I got a chill just calculating what the kid might do with a good pair of shoes.

"What'd it read?" the kid asked.

"Oh, 'round ninety," I said.

"Did I really hit ninety?"

"Yeah, but you always want to be careful where you throw the ball. That's the important thing. You hung that one a little too far over the plate. You've got natural speed so you want to think about *where* you're throwing the ball rather than how fast."

The kid nodded slowly and said, "Yeah, I been working on location with Teddy. But it helps if I have a batter up there."

The kid definitely had the speed so I put down the gun. "I'll get up there for you," I said.

"Thanks," he said.

I walked slowly back down to where Teddy stood with the catcher's mitt and picked up a bat. "How fast did it read, Nick?" he asked.

"Ninety-eight miles an hour," I said quietly.

"I knew it," he replied in a whisper.

I stood at the plate with the bat on my left shoulder and stared out at the kid. He looked big and impressive on the mound. Like a large truck with its doors open. I could feel Teddy crouch down along the inside corner just behind me. The big kid went into his windup and then exploded out of it. I picked up the ball about halfway down the chute and heard it smaaaack into the catcher's mitt. The pitch had good lateral movement on it and slammed in right under my hands across the inside corner.

Teddy flipped the ball back out to the kid and said, "That felt faster than the last one."

"How tall is he?" I asked.

"Almost six-five," Teddy said.

"And his weight?"

"That's a problem. Kid needs structure. A program. I can only do so much. Getting him to lay off the Big Macs and bend over and touch his toes is something else."

I nodded my understanding and looked out at the overweight kid on the mound in the red sweatshirt. Even with what I had just seen he'd be considered for some kind of a contract because we always looked for left-handers with speed. Throwing from the left side is preferred in the big leagues because the right field fences are usually shorter. With good speed and control it's that much harder to get around on the ball and pull it down the right field line into the stands. The kid also has the advantage of facing first base and keeping a runner close to the bag. That makes it harder to steal or even get a good lead. That means fewer stolen bases, more double plays, and fewer runs scored by the opposing team. The advantage of having a good left-handed pitcher out on the mound is enormous.

"Now I want you to throw the ball on the inside corner about knee-high with the same speed that you just gave me with the last one," I yelled out to him. Whether Shoe knew it or not I had asked for the pitch that either made the major league left-hander or broke him. The kid just smiled, went into his windup, and I tried to concentrate on when and where he released the ball. I never saw the ball until it got close to me and cut in at knee level along the inside corner. Then BAAAAMMM it hit the catcher's mitt.

"What kind of pitch did he throw?" I asked Teddy.

"A splitter."

"He got anything else?"

"I got him working on a fork ball but it's not ready."

"What about a change-up?"

"He's got one. But it needs work. He doesn't throw it with the same exact motion that he uses with the fast ball so a good hitter could read it and know it's coming."

"I'd still like to see it."

"Get ready," he said.

The kid took the sign from Teddy, and I watched him go

Part 1

HELLO, GOODBYE

into his windup. He came out of it with a slight hitch so I
adjusted my swing and hit a screaming line drive down the right
field line. The kid looked stunned as he watched the ball carom
off the building out in right field. Three of the kids ran out to
retrieve it.

"He's just got a different direction in his windup when he
throws his change-up. He comes into it from further out on the
mound," I said. "Just have him work on keeping that arm motion
in tight and it'll make all the difference especially if he uses it with
the splitter."

Teddy smiled and said, "Check."

"I can get one of the coaches to work with him. Show
him how to throw a few different change-ups."

"That oughta help," Teddy said calmly.

"I'd like to see how he looks with a right-handed batter in
there," I said. "Sometimes that kind of thing can be an enormous
problem. I've even seen it break a good left-hander."

"This kid doesn't have that kind of problem," he said
softly. I just stepped over homeplate and put the bat up on my
right shoulder to see how he'd deal with me from the other side.
He leaned forward and I could feel Teddy go into a crouch behind
me.

Then the kid did something I had never seen in all my
years in baseball. He flipped that weird homemade baseball glove
onto his left hand and went into his windup from the other side.
Before I realized what had happened he fired a knee-high pitch
straight down the middle at about ninety-five miles an hour with
his *right* arm.

"What the hell did that kid just do?" I said quietly to
Teddy.

"I wanted you to see it rather than try and explain it," he
said and flipped the ball back out to the mound.

"Does he have the same kind of control from both sides?"

"Yeah, but I think he's a little faster from the left."

"Let's see his splitter from the right side," I said in quiet
shock. Teddy knelt down. The kid took the sign, went into his
windup, and spun out of it in a red blur. I picked up the ball
somewhere near homeplate and watched it hook sharply in under
the narrow part of the bat and slaaaam into the catcher's mitt.
The row of dark-haired kids in the stands cheered wildly.

"Put a jacket on him. We're finished for now," I said.

22

"Sure you've seen enough?"

"It's getting cold. I don't want him to tighten up. Besides, what else is there?"

"He's a pretty good fielder. Ain't a bad hitter either."

I held up my hands, smiled numbly at him, and he trotted out to tell the kid that he could go and get a hamburger or just head home. The tryout had ended. What I'd just seen could turn the game of baseball upside down and inside out. Take it up another notch. A pitcher like that could double his output of pitches per game simply by being able to throw the ball over ninety miles an hour with either arm, and also have an advantage over any switch-hitter. I didn't think there were any rules in the book to cover it. And at this point I didn't care.

I could see Teddy talking with him out on the mound before they headed back towards me. The kid stuck out his hand and I took it. "Thanks for coming, Mr. Costa," he said. "Nice meeting you."

"I'll be in touch," I said quietly, "but you'll probably have to come down to Phoenix for a few days, if that's all right?"

The kid didn't answer but Teddy nodded and said, "I made appointments with some other scouts, Nick." I must've looked surprised at what he said because he followed up quickly with, "I didn't know whether the powers down in Phoenix were open for a new pitcher like Shoe here."

"They're always open for left-handers with speed," I said, not mentioning the incredible fact that the kid threw from both sides.

"There's a storm coming in. You better put your jacket on before you tighten up," Teddy said, and the kid threw a half-hearted wave to the both of us and headed back across the street to the church.

"What scouts did you make appointments with?" I asked and tried not to sound annoyed.

"Tom Purvis and Steve Merton," Teddy said and looked away. Then he handed me the catcher's mask and said, "The kid doesn't think he did very well."

"He did fine. Better than fine."

"That line drive you hit made him think he failed the tryout."

"Did you tell him I knew his change-up was coming?"

"Yeah, but he didn't believe me."

"The young ones are like that," I said and tried to change the subject. "How big a foot does he really have?"

"Twelve...twelve and a half wide and still growing."

Teddy started to take off the catcher's gear and I said, "Tell him I'll set up a tryout for him down in Phoenix right away. I'm not sure the pitching coach is in town but I could get the owner to come out and take a look."

Teddy didn't answer. When he finished taking off the shin guards we started back across the infield together. I had never talked business with Teddy before and I felt uncomfortable. Things weren't the same in Tuba City as they were in Tucson. I didn't know what to say. Teddy's silence seemed to make the situation clear, and I couldn't help feeling betrayed by my old friend.

"I think this kid should be on the Arizona team," I said as casually as I could. "It's where he belongs."

"Because he's an Indian?" Teddy said.

I hesitated and then said, "No...because he's a Navajo."

Teddy smiled and looked at me with the same kind of suspicious stare that the pale horse had given me on the way in. I felt even more like the intruding outsider as I waited for his answer.

"I've gotta do what's right for the kid," he finally said.

I had to be careful of what I said. The tryout had been the shortest and fastest I ever conducted. Something told me that Teddy knew it'd go that way even before I got there. He'd dragged me all the way up to Tuba City just to put me into a bidding situation with the competition.

I opened the trunk of the car in silence. Teddy dropped in the catcher's equipment while one of the boys put back the box of baseballs. I repacked the speed gun, slid in the bat, and stood there for a long, uncertain moment in front of the open trunk. Teddy didn't look at me. When he started to close the trunk I stopped him and took out my checkbook. "The kid deserves a deal," I said, and quickly wrote out my personal check to Harold "Big Shoe" Bromley for two thousand dollars, and on the back of the check I wrote, "I knew your change-up was coming otherwise I wouldn't have gotten near it."

I handed the check to Teddy and said, "Cancel those appointments with Tom and Steve. I'll set up another tryout for the kid as fast as I can."

Teddy looked at my personal check and smiled at what I

had written on the back. "I really never made those appointments with Tom and Steve," he said, but didn't crack his usual smile.

"Then why did you tell me that?" I asked.

"I needed to give the kid something. Something real. Something of value." He stopped talking and looked up at me. "This kid needs that," he said. "All these kids need that."

I began to understand what had just happened. I might be an outsider in Tuba City but Teddy was an outsider too. He'd always been the outsider. And for the first time I knew that was the look I'd seen in his eyes without ever realizing it.

I smiled at him and said, "Make sure the kid gets a new pair of sneakers and a baseball glove with some of that money." He nodded his understanding and I said, "But don't cash it until Thursday."

He laughed and seemed to relax. Then he waved my check in the air and said, "This'll make the kid happy. He can call himself a *pro* now."

"It'll make me happy too," I said and handed the Navajo kids the box of baseballs they had just put back into the trunk.

"You don't have to do that," Teddy said quietly.

I gave the kids a couple of bats to go with the balls and said, "Let's just say it's an investment for the future and leave it at that." The row of dark-haired boys looked up expectantly for Teddy's approval.

"I'm going to need your help with this kid Shoe," I said.

"I'm glad you understand that," he answered quietly.

I started to get into the car but then extended my hand, and it surprised Teddy because in all the years we had known each other we never shook hands. The big Navajo smile came across his chiseled face and he opened his arms and embraced me. For the first time I felt close to him. Like a friend.

"We'll see you in Phoenix," he said.

I started the car and the kids ran down Moenave Street behind me waving the bats and balls. I made the turn, headed out past the burned out pickup, and the "GO WARRIORS" sign. When I glanced into the rearview mirror I saw the pale horse nibbling contentedly on the sagebrush. If my luck held out I'd make the low desert before the storm hit.

The Woman's Field Guide to Survival

I have seen the chrysalis
of the painted lady. Her
brown house is upside down
before walls crack and fall away
from the green, globe thistle leaf,
from her butterfly body slick as mine.
Motionless
we hand onto the damp hours before dawn

and count the high cost
of a single wrong choice,
a split-second indiscretion

before our colors emerge: our camouflage complete.
Our wings tipped with eyespots expand, a burst
of pink and purple woven lace across our backs
strong as any grocery sack that holds our sun.

I have seen the painted lady
perch on goldenrod
and heard her wings rustle against my lips
as she wrangles the wind with me.

We hear the whisk and whoosh
as the blue jay tilts his beak
and dives for us.
He may get one

eyespot but we still see
the everlastings, white puffs
of baby's breath and moon-red
crests of cockscomb. I have seen

the painted lady
lay her froth of eggs and leave
me alone in wetlands

where I stand on one leg
in the warm shallows
like a blue heron. I choose

fish words that streak
through waves and I wait
for one perfect trout.

– Carol Carpenter

reserved for senses

i

at the river
in the mouth of the river
at the gloaming
at the gloaming in the mouth of the river

we shined
the brink of tide
distilled and diffused
a trance
in the river

biology surges
bold and indifferent
as the storming yellow star
throws fiery insults

ii

jittery and out of sequence
we taste the moon
as eyelids lap salt
tongues blink
hands tremble in the sound
of it all

– Dan Sicoli

A Poem Speaks to the Poet

Make of your elbows small pebbles
rolling the river bottom, a fierce and pummeling sweep.

If you will, build of your limbs and trunk
the supple breast and weight of the water.

Render of your hands eels,
your ears twin leeches sucking sound,
those rough-heeled feet   two swift fish
flicking the shadowed pull of current.

Of eyes and mouth shape glints and echoes,
sunlight and voices under the bridge.

If you can make of yourself water's muscle,
then perhaps I can float:

lay my head where the shoulder of the river rounds,
where the heft of it bends and pools,

hear the river's shifting joints,   taste summer
licked from the lips of a swimmer.

Be sure to tell all the tales—   the laughter and the drownings—
what you have taken and what you leave behind:

whole lives, wide banks strewn with smooth stones,
the yellow foam of pollen painting the shore.

– Christina Hutchins

Cinderella Vérité

I was never locked upstairs; that's a fiction.
And there were never any cutesy talking mice:
everyone knows that mice don't talk—and after all,
in this house, I'm the one who traps them.

When the prince's gofer came for the maiden
whose foot would fit that shoe, I never tried it on—
and I never raced downstairs with its dusty, cracked mate
to prove I was the one: I'd never kept it.

The prince was stoned. I closed my eyes
and clung to him; the other dancers
twirled past us laughing ...
the musky smell of pumpkin

floated off my skin—my rough, sore hands
just inches from his face,
those ugly years of cinder-crud
jammed beneath my nails—I didn't care.

But then he rammed me to him hard—
drove his tongue so deep I learned the hardness of his heart
as those ghastly Steuben chandeliers
swirled about our heads in jangling swarms ...

Ice-sheets of terror slid down my spine.
I hiked up my petticoats higher than sin,
kicked off those damned shoes
one by one mid-spin—

all the better to run from him.

– Gabrielle LeMay

Pursuit of Happiness

pursue   perhaps to catch
if not caught   despair
how much time allotted for the chase
hours   days   years
if caught
grasp   rein in   hold tight
then to guard
lest it escape
and the hunt commence again
better yet   breathe   slowly   deeply
smile   be open
happiness may well find its way

– Jeanne Norwin

Catherine Gentile

A Teaspoon of Perfection

I shoveled ash into the dented bucket by my wood stove, hoping I looked as if this were exactly what I wanted to do first thing on my day off. Balder had stopped in on his way to work, most likely to continue last night's conversation. I distracted him with fresh coffee.

"Want me to help you with that?" he asked and set his cup on the floor. He was red-faced, gray-haired, and at this moment, intense.

"Another time, I'm almost done," I said.

"You make a lousy advertisement, Katie Shields."

"Excuse me?" I asked, snaking my head around.

"How can I tell our customers wood stoves are for emergencies when you're burning wood by the armload?" His voice trailed off and I could feel him staring at my hindquarter, probably noticing how much it looked like a horse that was about to kick.

"Let's say I'm addicted to the crackle of burning wood. Besides, what are you going to do, tell everyone?" Life was much simpler when I ran the business solo, before I'd bought my second oil truck and convinced Philip Balder, my long time drinking buddy, he could spare a few hours from his horse farm to drive it. But he had surprised me.

"Employee isn't good enough," he'd said. "I want to be your equal partner."

I shook my head, offered him a forty-nine percent share instead.

Balder had paused, seemed to be thinking. I was about to step back and give him the kind of space I would want if I were making a life-altering decision when he grabbed my hand and gave it a shake. We drove from the office to The Lobster's Claw, on Route 1, outside of Ellsworth, to celebrate. He took a napkin from the bar and sketched a picture of Leah, my Irish Wolfhound, in a full gallop. "How about changing the name of the company?" he asked, and printed, 'Balder and the Bitch'."

"Touché, very funny," I'd said. "But forty-nine percent is still the best I can do."

I stood, brushed the ash from my hands and turned

toward Balder. "I suppose I could use the furnace, especially while Mom's visiting."

She must have heard us because she came out of the guestroom in her T-shirt and spandex leggings, carrying a pair of Nikes. She shivered, took her sweatshirt from the back of the sofa and slipped it over her L'Oreal blond curls. "I bet Balder would caulk those leaky windows, if only you'd ask," she said.

Balder raised one of his tufted eyebrows into a v-shape and exchanged glances with my mother. "Whenever you're ready, Katie."

"I'll take care of it," I said, annoyed at the conspiracy that had just begun.

He leaned over, cupped his hand to Mom's ear and whispered real loud. "The way I figure it, if she won't take me up on my offer, then I haven't done a good job of asking."

They giggled while I closed my eyes, irritated but grateful to Balder for coaxing a smile from Mom. It had been three months since she'd phoned with that close-to-hysterical tone in her voice to tell me Dad had died of a massive coronary and it was good to hear her laugh.

"Anything new with Balder?" Mom asked, after he'd left. I'd made the mistake of telling her that Balder had hired a manager for his farm so he could spend more time at our office and that he wanted to marry me.

I tried to sound casual. "Not a thing. Balder's still my business partner, nothing more."

Later that day, Mom and I were on our way home from the health club, bouncing along on the dirt road to my house when Mom put her hands on the dashboard and said, "There's the Blueberry Fortress." That's what she'd named my two-story home, built like a moatless castle, by an eccentric architect, in the middle of a blueberry patch by Cadillac Mountain. The first floor is as open as a bowling alley, with a spiral staircase leading up a tower to the most beautiful spot in the house, my master bedroom. Leah and I sleep there beside the sliding glass doors. Each morning, after I open my eyes to the bristly-faced mountain, we step onto the deck to watch the goldfinches and chickadees darting from the nearby spruces to my feeders, and back.

"But there is something missing," she said, twisting her wedding band.

I braced myself. "What's that, Mom?"

"A man." She got that starry look, the one that came before a mother-daughter moment, and said, "You can have all sorts of things, Katie, a truck, a business, a house, but they'll never replace a man."

Static whistled from her hearing aid and Mom fiddled with the dial behind her ear then pointed to Leah, waiting by the mailbox at the end of the driveway. She ran alongside us, keeping pace with the truck's twenty-five miles per hour, her ivory head level with my window, her tongue spewing spit. "She gallops like a miniature horse," Mom said.

She seemed delightfully childish, and I wondered about this becoming a problem. Her doctor had assured me she didn't have Alzheimer's. "Short term memory deficit" was the term he'd used, but it made me want to weep, knowing all I could do was hang on tight as Mom yo-yoed between confusion and knowing exactly what she was doing.

"I wonder if Balder misses his horses," Mom said.

My hands tightened around the steering wheel. While she worried about him, I wondered if he'd lose interest if I didn't maintain the independent filly routine. Wondered what he'd do if he knew it didn't come naturally, and that I had to work damn hard to avoid becoming like my mother had been, harnessed to her man.

I parked the truck by the granite ledge on the side of the house. Leah pressed her spotted nose against the window. Her breath froze on the glass as we listened to predictions of our first snow. "A nor'easter," the announcer's voice said. As Mom started talking about Balder, I turned off the engine and said, "Please, not again."

She looked down at her hands and nodded. This was her first visit without my father and she seemed wobbly, like a kid trying to balance her new bike without its training wheels. A kid who needed me to keep one hand on the handlebar, the other on the seat, and run beside her, ready to catch her, if she were to fall.

When I let Leah into the house, she bolted up the spiral staircase and howled for me to open the doors to the deck. "Go ahead, guard the fortress," I said, and she stepped outside. The air had that damp, cold smell that comes before it snows, and my nose told me we're about to have a storm.

I left Leah outside and sank into my waterbed. It'd been the first thing I bought when I left my husband. After eighteen years on the same mattress, I'd asked him to buy a new one, like the ones advertised on TV. He refused, said I needed to stop believing everything I heard. The water in the individual tubes made a lonely sloshing sound as I rolled toward my bedside stand, lifted the phone and dialed the office.

Balder answered, "Blueberry Oil Distributors." Lyle Lovett, his favorite CD, played in the background. Mom and I had once argued about how hard it would be for a woman my age to get used to living with someone else. She assured me it'd be easy to let Balder's tastes and habits become my own. "First, he'll try to teach you the Texas two-step and you'll wonder if you'll ever stop tripping over his feet. Then one day, you'll find yourself gliding along, humming his favorite tune."

I pictured his lanky six-foot-two in his survival suit, unzipped to the waist, steel toe boots on the desk. Balder named the new customers who'd signed up for oil delivery and went on to tell me how Fibber, the dog down the street from the office, had been hit by a car. "He's okay. I brought him to Dr. Carly's," he said, and described the ordeal.

There was a hollow clunk on the other end of the line; Balder's feet had dropped to the floor. He'd changed the CD to Tommy Makem's, *The Lark in the Morning*. The band had played that song during my father's retirement party at the Portland Country Club, three weeks before his heart attack. Two hundred people applauded when I introduced my gift: Jamie McCallum, Pipe Major, in full dress regalia. His green and blue plaid kilt swished to the beat of "Minstrel Boy" while he marched back and forth in front of my father. Dad stood at attention and, as his favorite, "Bonnie Lass," droned, he stared at me.

Tears glistened on Dad's face, and I'd wanted to go to him. Wanted to tell him that thirty years and one wrecked marriage had given me plenty of opportunity to compare my ex-husband's need for other women with my father's need for my mother. And that, by comparison, he'd come out on the positive side of my equation. But the piper played a strathspey, and someone called for Dad and Mom to lead the dancing, and my chance got lost in the next reel.

And I thought about last night and how I chanced losing again. Balder had wanted to talk about us, but I said, "It's only been four years since the divorce; my life is just beginning to feel right." I knew Balder was "right" but didn't know if he'd be perfect. Didn't know if I could tolerate not having perfection this time, didn't want to risk exploring it.

Balder stopped talking and I chatted about what great shape Mom was in. "By the way, I wondered what you thought of having a party tomorrow night for my mother. It'll be her seventy-fifth birthday. I'm going to make lasagna and a cake."

"You think she's in the mood? It's only been three months since she buried your father." Balder sounded somber, weighted with duty, like the time I'd complained to him about my ex-husband leaving me alone, hemorrhaging after my hysterectomy.

Balder told me I'd never have to worry, he wasn't that kind of man. "Prove it," I'd said, as we hiked up the carriage trails in Acadia National Park. Balder had left college to take a job, he told me, his green eyes sad and still. I knew he'd never married, and I asked him why. He called the co-ed who'd lied about taking the pill a gold-digger. I imagined Balder at the end of his weekly visits, leaving his little boy at his mother's door. Then later, at his desk in his farmhouse, writing a check, one each month, until his son had finished his degree.

I got angry. At that sponging bitch, at my father's leaving my mother so unexpectedly, at Balder's telling me what to do, and most of all, at myself, for being so terrified that what's happening to my mother is what is going to happen to me.

I snapped into the phone, "We're not going to rock 'n roll, stupid. It's going to be a quiet dinner party." As soon as the words came out, I wanted to snatch them back. But it was too late, and besides, I could use some distance between Balder and me. But the gap felt bigger than I'd expected.

On the other end of the phone, Balder blew out smoke, prolonged and emphatic, like the chimney on a factory at quitting time.

"I'm sorry, I shouldn't have said that. It's just that ..."

"Don't worry Katie, I've had sand kicked in my face before. I'll be the blind man, if that makes you happy. But do me a favor, stop pretending my opinion matters." He sighed. "A party is just what your mother needs. Is that what you want to hear?"

I slammed the phone down because he was right, that was exactly what I wanted to hear. If paying attention to Balder were first on my list, I wouldn't put him off every time he got close to asking me to marry him. Wouldn't be so skittish about putting myself in a situation where I might become, once again, the kind of wife my mother had been.

Round and round, my hand glided along the smooth, black railing on the spiral staircase into the kitchen. What if Balder swapped his hopes of life with me for one with someone smart enough to know that Balder is the name of the Norse god of wisdom and light; someone who'd treat him accordingly?

"Why shouldn't he find someone else?" I asked aloud, amazed at the words' sickening effect. I imagined life without him and felt as if I'd lost something important, a leg, an eye, my soul perhaps.

This last thought scared me. Grateful for a party to get ready for, I opened the pantry, balanced several cans of tomatoes in the crook of my arm, and hurried to the counter just as they rolled off. The farm girl's picture on the fifteen-ounce can appeared then disappeared as it careened towards the bud vase and pink carnations Balder had given Mom. I stepped to the right, hand extended, ready to scoop it up, when my ankle turned beneath me and I tumbled to the floor.

"Damn you, Leah," I bellowed. Pain shot through my ankle as I hurled her foot-long chew-bone at the wall.

Leah threw herself against the deck doors while my mother's slippered footsteps scurried from her bedroom to my side. "What happened?" she asked, and inspected my ankle. "You need an ice pack." Her voice was clear and in control.

With my hand hooked on the sink, I hauled myself up, my weight on my good foot. I swung the other up on the counter, untied my sneaker and rested my ankle in a puddle of water. Pink carnations were strewn, as if by flower girls, around my foot.

"It's swelling," I muttered from behind clenched teeth.

My mother unloaded a tray of ice cubes into a dishtowel, tied it into a knot and settled the icepack on my ankle, then slipped a chair under me. "Keep your foot there, I'll get a stool." She hurried off to her bedroom and returned with it and pillows from her bed. She stacked them and lowered my leg.

"Here's a naproxen tablet for the inflammation," she said, and reached into her pocket for an oval pill tinted Robin's egg blue. She ran the faucet and handed me a glass of water, then the pill.

"Thanks, Mom," I whispered. Exhaustion tugged at me, and I gave in to it, unsure if I was relieved more by my mother's presence or by her being focused enough to take care of me. I placed my elbow on the counter and rested my head.

The door of the wood stove creaked open. One log thumped against another, then landed on the grate. Embers flared, like disturbed bees, then settled into their work. Cast iron clinked against cast iron, sealing in the warmth from the heart of the stove, overpowering the cool breezes that had crept, uninvited, into my fortress.

Leah quieted down, and I could hear Mom speaking in the other room. She stopped for a moment, then said, "Yes Balder, that would be very helpful." The rest of her words blurred as I fell asleep.

When I awoke the ice pack, now in a crinkling plastic bag, fell to the floor. I twisted around toward the stove. My ankle throbbed. Propped on one elbow, I squinted first at my feet at the other end of the sofa, then at the footstool by my head.

"Mom, how'd I get to the sofa?" I asked, my voice little and young. I checked the footstool to see if Mom had left me a drink; Balder's fleece vest was there instead.

Mom and Balder poked their heads out from the other side of the brick hearth. They wore identical aprons; blue canvas with white lettering, *Blueberry Oil Distributors*.

"That was quite a tumble you took," Balder said, and knelt by my side.

"It was so stupid," I began, but Balder put his fingers over my lips. He tasted sweet, like basil.

"It was an accident," he said, his tone firm. "But when I found you passed out on the counter, I got scared."

"Really?"

Mom handed me a glass of ginger ale. "How're you feeling?" Confused, I wanted to say. I clasped Balder's hand, let him pull me upright then took the glass from Mom.

Balder lifted the afghan from my feet and inspected the damage. "Looks like a bad sprain," he said, his face tensed with concern. "I've called the emergency room; they're expecting us in half an hour."

The following evening was Mom's seventy-fifth birthday and I sat on the sofa, disappointed I hadn't gotten a gift for her. Years ago, I'd bought her bath towels with enormous sunflowers on them. She tucked them in her linen closet, behind a stack of her solid green ones as if to say, 'gifts need to fit the person, not the giver'. I'd learned that finding the perfect match meant loosening my definition of perfection and wondered if I'd been able to go shopping today, what I would have chosen.

"Can I help, Mrs. Shields?" Balder asked. He leaned against the counter, sipping beer from a frosty mug; an unexpected jealousy ran through me.

"Everything's ready." Mom pulled the lasagna out of the oven and the aroma of herbs and spices filled the house. I marveled. She'd coped with my injury and made our dinner.

Balder popped ice cubes into a glass. "Who's having a Shirley Temple?" he asked, and shot me a consoling grin. His slender face was a wind-kissed red and his silver hair ponytailed at the nape of his neck. "Don't worry Katie, you won't need to take codeine for long."

He handed me a glass of ginger ale, kissed my forehead and said, "Your Mom and I are going to bring the table in here so you won't have to move."

I smiled a woozy smile, content to let him care for me. It was a risk associated with taking this painkiller, one little white pill every four hours. May impair judgement, but I didn't mind. Even with drug-saturated eyes, I could see the happiness on Balder's weathered face. The brownish hue in his green-gray eyes was soft, confident, that of a man who knew he belonged. Who wasn't afraid of the "for worse" part of "for better or for worse." Who wasn't threatened by what might be. Who was comfortable with what is.

"It's snowing," Mom said from the kitchen.

"Thanks for being here," I said, and reached for Balder's oil-stained hand.

Moments later, Balder and Mom inched their way around the hearth, their arms taut, he squatting to keep the table balanced between them. Then Mom lifted the lasagna on a hot plate as if she were carrying the platter for a Boar's Head celebration. Balder raised an imaginary trumpet and sang, "Dum, da-da, daaa."

I swallowed hard, wasn't used to anyone going out of his way for me, except now that I thought about it, that's all Balder had ever done.

He poured Chianti, my favorite, into all the glasses, except mine. "Do you want some grape juice?" he asked.

I tried to sound stoic. "Someone's got to stay sober." We

both laughed, until Mom said, "It was cute but nothing to get hysterical over," and we laughed even harder. It was my first laugh since my accident and sharing it with Balder felt good.

After dinner, the table looked as if locusts had landed. Half the lasagna was gone and the bread and salad had disappeared. Balder cleared the glasses, grasping one stem between his thumb and index finger and the others between his knuckles. They sparkled like baubles.

The lights flickered and the refrigerator motor sputtered. "Storm must be bringing down the power lines," Balder said. The northeast winds whipped pine boughs against the clapboards and the lights flickered, then the house went black, except for the glow from the wood stove.

"What's happening?" Mom asked, panic in her voice.

"Balder's getting the lantern. It's going to be all right."

A soft radiance filled the room as the god of Light entered and lowered the lantern to the table. Mom's face glowed and she whispered, "Remember how your father used to tell me to make a wish whenever the power went out? If it came on within the hour, he'd say my wish had been granted." She paused. "It's too bad your father had a trial this week, he would have loved this."

Balder and I exchanged looks. His eyes locked on mine. Now you know, I thought. I panicked, wanted to go to Mom, but couldn't reach my crutches. My eyes skittered between Balder and Mom.

"Mom? Dad's not at a trial."

"I know that, Katie. Sometimes, I pretend he's still with us. It's silly, but it makes it easier to tolerate the ache."

"You're right, Mrs. Shields. Sometimes when I'm on the farm repairing fence posts, I imagine working shoulder to shoulder with my son."

I felt sorry for Mom, but sorrier for Balder. He fathered a son, but never had one; asked for an equal partnership but got one percent less; offered me love, knowing the most I could give was a teaspoon of perfection.

"I'm ready to make my wish now," Mom said, and closed her eyes.

I closed mine and thought about giving. I've never been able to find the perfect gift. Maybe that's why we need lots of birthdays, so we'll have another chance to figure out how to make the person we love happy. Eventually we learn to celebrate whatever fits the person, and sometimes we get lucky, and find ourselves loving the gift, too. Mom sighed. I opened my eyes; I knew what my gift would be.

Balder burst into the room with a cake lit like a torch and set it in front of Mom. He pretended to look for the key of C on an imaginary pitch pipe, hummed it and started singing "Happy Birthday."

But Mom looked lost, left out, as if she didn't get the punch line to a joke. She looked from Balder to me, her smile timid, her penciled eyebrows furrowed in confusion. Leah howled as we sang, "Happy Birthday dear Mom Mrs. Shields ..." I kept smiling, even though I wanted to cry. For her, comfort came from knowing what to expect. Perhaps that's why she was so certain that a marriage to Balder would work out; in her seventy-five years, she'd developed a sense of what a woman could expect from a man like Balder, and to her, it was okay. I pointed to her and mouthed, "It's for you."

Mom's face brightened and she blew out the flames from seventy-six candles: seventy-five and one to grow on. "Those roses remind me of the ones that used to come on cakes from Martin's Bakery in Portland. Do you remember, Katie?" Mom asked.

"Um," I said, savoring a fingertip of frosting.

"Remember how you used to peel back the petals on the rosebuds?"

"Remember how I used to wish the bakery would hide tiny gifts in them?" I slid the rosebud from the cake and sucked the buttery frosting from its stem, then pushed the first petal back, the second, and the third.

The lantern flickered on the glittering rosebud. Something dropped with a "cah-chink." A dime store ring, the kind with the adjustable shank and a pretend diamond with gaudy, heart-shaped rubies, one on either side, had landed on my plate.

"What's this?" I asked. Mom held her fingertips in prayer position over her mouth and nose. Her hearing aid whistled.

Balder dragged the table back, peeling away my armor, leaving me exposed and vulnerable. He picked up the ring with his thumb and index finger and fell to his knees on one side of my outstretched leg. His honest, round eyes peered into mine and he held his ring in his Light.

I knew what he was doing, but was distracted by the corners of his mouth twitching, waiting for my signal to release his smile. I didn't want Balder to wait any more. I reached out and traced his lips.

Balder looked silly, solid, and wonderful, and we laughed when he tried to slip the ring on my finger. He stopped, adjusted it and slid it over my knuckle. His fingertips traced the freckles on my cheeks, leftovers from my girlhood, perhaps pretending if he landed on the right one, I'd award him the key to my fortress.

His wiry beard sent loving messages up and down my neck. I combed my fingers through his hair and started humming. The logs in the stove shifted into new forms and I glanced at our shadows dancing a slow dance to the beat of embers settling on the grate.

Pastoral With Birds

How can you sleep? Swallows
screech around the lodge,
to say, not room enough
for little ones. Their tough

territorial swoops
through lattice tangles blotch
the day. A robin scoots
down a tire track, stuffs

a morsel in its fat mate's
mouth. You rouse up. Two
males vie for a crusty
beetle, one flies, one pecks

water from a shrinking pool.
You slink on tip toes
across the cabin floor,
bite my bare neck.

– Parker Towle

Mirror

Your tongue reaches my mind—
Invisible fingers open and close
fold like wings—
brushing my closed eyelids
Harp strings rise
in the motion of notes
pressed in Braille
A silent swing—
Amygdala trembles breaking like a flag

– Jimmie Margaret Gilliam

What May Come to You in Sleep

Far off in the fields,
on the hummocks of grass
yellowed with the last
sheets of sunlight, they appear,
brown coats glowing.
Like fretful thoughts
before an uneasy sleep,
the deer stamp,
show challenge in their chests.
Nearby, the eye of the pond
closes and blunted wedges
of heads turn in the darkness
and watch. The eyelid flickers
and waves wet the shore.
Heedless of their course
two deer bolt, become
two wild thoughts, dispelled
only by small cries.
A buck leaps from the field,
stands riveted in the path
and regards your fear.
Restless and pursued,
you awake.

– James Sedwick

Part 2

The third grade has its own oral tradition

Claudia Montague Wheatley

Hello, Goodbye

We called her the Amazing Disappearing Baby.

From the day she could crawl, we had to keep an eye on Meg every minute or risk losing her. We *did* lose her, many times. At the mall. At the lake. In our own house. Meg got away from me so many times at the supermarket, the clerks all knew her by sight and the regular shoppers knew me by name; I was the frantic lady sprinting to the front of the store as the PA system blared, "Will the mother of Meg Wheatley please report to the Customer Service Desk, please?" She was a born explorer and utterly fearless. When she was three, she easily eluded the inexperienced teenagers hired to mind the children during a family reunion and went next door to see what the neighbors were up to. "She wanted to have dinner with us, but we thought we'd better bring her back," the neighbors explained, half amused, half alarmed.

As the years went by, and the siblings we had hoped to supply her with failed to materialize, we were frequently warned about the perils of Only Child Syndrome: the desire to wrap the precious singling in cotton batting and protect her from the world. Our advisors could have saved their breath. It's not that we never felt that desire; it's that Meg wouldn't go along with it. She had to learn everything by herself, usually the hard way. Don't play with strange dogs, we said, and the minute she was alone with another inexperienced teenager she approached a strange dog that nearly relieved her of her nose, occasioning her first surgery. Don't jump on the furniture, we said, and she built a mountain of chairs and couches and climbed it and fell, breaking her right arm so badly that a second operation was necessary. Don't ride your horse alone in the upper fields, we said, and she did, of course, and when a herd of deer burst out of the underbrush and scared him, he tossed her and she fell off, breaking the wrist on her other arm.

Each experience left her a little more sober, a little more careful, but ultimately unfazed. A week after the fall from her horse, with her wrist in a cast, Meg rode that same horse in a show and won a blue ribbon.

With all that energy and independence roiling inside her, it was probably inevitable that Meg's teen years would be . . . something of a trial. Given her history of accidents resulting from faulty judgment, her father and I were leery of affording her the freedom she felt entitled to as a 13-, 14-, and 15-year-old. The battles were frequent and fierce, marked by intensifying cycles of defiance and punishment. Finally we sought the assistance of a professional counselor. We expected her to explain to Meg why Mom and Dad knew best. Instead, she ordered us to back off. She needs some freedom, the traitor said. Give it to her, or she will take it herself—and that could be bad news all around.

Grudgingly we backed off a little. Meg rewarded us by demonstrating unsuspected reserves of self-restraint and maturity. We backed off a little more. She responded by growing up before our eyes. It was simple and awe-some; not "awesome" in the slangy sense, but in the sense of literally inspiring awe. Where did this incredible young woman come from?

From there flowed other decisions and changes, the kind I thought would be impossible to sanction, but which turned out to be rather easy after all. She got a car—an ancient Volvo 240D, ugly as an Earth Shoe, but roadworthy and reliable, and she drove it with caution and care. She got a job, and grumbled about the stupid customers stupid bosses stupid co-workers but reported for every shift on time and in uniform. Motivated by the desire "to finally get the hell out of there," she buckled down in high school and made high honor roll, as well as editing the literary magazine, presiding over the art club, singing in chorus, and nailing down big roles in all the musicals. She picked out a college—not our first choice, but it was her choice after all, and she did the research, filled out the applications, and made all the arrangements for a weekend campus visit.

So when the day came to pack the cars and take her to Westchester County, it felt at once surreal and like a trip we had been preparing for all those 17-plus years. We the parents were thrilled and distraught. Our daughter was an achingly sweet Halfling, teetering back and forth on the tipping point between adult and child. She drove her Volvo by herself; but seemed grateful that I rode with her instead of her dad. She wanted to sign in and fetch her own key; but stood by passively as I smoothed the new sheets on her bed. She could hardly wait to get rid of us, largely I think to get the sharp pain of parting out of the way as quickly as possible.

We went home to our empty nest and the reproachful gaze of our dog, who clearly felt that we had carelessly mislaid her pal. I spent a couple of weeks alternately battling anxiety and relief. I remembered my aunt staggering up the stairs with a basket of laundry and announcing that she had never worked so hard in her life as she had since she'd had kids. I was offended: Surely raising children was an unalloyed pleasure! I had been a mother less than two months when I grasped the truth of her remark. Even if it entailed no physical labor—and it does, it does!—motherhood would be exhausting because the work of mothering is unremitting; there are no weekends or holidays, no time when you aren't conscious that a little piece of yourself is wandering around somewhere, unprotected and at the mercy of an uncaring universe. At 18, under the semi-parental protection of a college, Meg seemed at once safe and completely vulnerable. She was off my hands and on her own. (Did she take a raincoat? would she wear it?) There was an immediate reduction in laundry and the grocery bill. (Was she eating right? leaving her clothes in the laundry room for others to steal?) I could relax with the knowledge of a job well done. (Did I ever teach her about sorting darks and whites? did she know how to access her home bank account?)

The weeks dragged by. I barely turned around twice and Meg was back again for winter break, hauling a laundry bag the size of a small pony behind her. She was bursting with health. She was thrilled to be home, grateful for home cooking and a certain amount of fussing.

A week passed, and she began to chafe under the house rules. No loud television after midnight? Call if you're not going to be home by nine? CLEAN YOUR ROOM??? When did we become so rigid? She experimented with insisting on her rights as an adult, while maintaining some of the privileges (spending money, subsidized health and beauty products, laundry service) of childhood. We were renegotiating the terms of our relationship at this newest and strangest stage, and it did not all go smoothly. But enough of it did so that when she left for spring semester, she felt inspired to leave us a note.

"It was fun being home again," she enthused, "and it was great to see you both." It was a prompt and polite thank-you note to a host, of the sort written by a young person of great confidence and good manners. Am I proud? Do I see this as evidence of a job well done? Am I getting a little tearful just thinking about it?

Yes.

Shakespeare in the Third Grade

While scholars squabble about great books
And debate the canon,
The third grade has its own oral tradition
Of tales told on the playground,
Under the slide, beside the swing,
At a table in the cafeteria,
Or whispered when the teacher turns toward the board.
Like the one where the boy recites his ABC's,
Skipping the letter "P"
Because, as the teacher discovers,
It has just run down his leg:

A tale we all heard or repeated
Standing in line for the lavatory,
Or even our parents, or theirs, heard,
Preserved not in the amber of a Norton Anthology,
But in the shimmering ephemeral spring pool
Of a third grade mind.

Perhaps Shakespeare himself,
Nudged by a classmate,
Smiled and listened intently at eight years,
Had an early laugh at language,
And first discovered
That words are slippery signifiers
Even as they run down our legs.

– Gordon Crock

Election Day

Just before they leave to vote
her husband briefs her
on the best man for each job,
president, congressman,
state treasurer and attorney general.
She nods as she pretends to listen
to his spiel, no room for discussion,
the newspaper spread on the kitchen
table in front of him, a red pen
in his hand as he circles the best choices.
He'll not have her canceling out
his precious votes this year.

She enters the booth clutching
the folded newspaper with its red ovals
pressed so hard into the paper they can
be seen from the backside page.
When she pulls the curtain closed
she tucks the newspaper under her arm
and in that quiet privacy that reminds her
of a confessional, she hides from him
but not from her conscience. Her finger
runs down the list of names, finds
a "Beth" and stops, finds a "Susan"
and stops, finds a "Nancy."

When she opens the curtain, he is
waiting for her, already done himself,
in and out fast, the same as when
he goes to confession.

– Mary Laufer

Maggie Lamond Simone

Moms and Bads

I consider myself a good mother. I'm intelligent, educated, young enough to read the right books, and old enough to use common sense. I have a toddler son and an infant daughter whom I love more than life. They are well fed and well dressed. They have toys, but not too many, and watch TV, but not too much. I don't spank, and I try, sometimes successfully, not to yell.

I'm not a perfect mom, but I always thought I was a good one. Then one day I broke my daughter's leg.

I was at the top of the stairs, baby on my hip, and when I took the first step my foot went out from under me. The next thing I knew, I was flat on my back on the stairs with her leg caught underneath me.

I didn't protect her. I didn't pull her around in front of me as I was landing, which would have spared her leg and prevented her from landing so forcefully that her head bounced. I didn't do anything to protect my child. I didn't have time.

Nor do I know why it happened. I wasn't hurrying. I wasn't upset. I was just going down the stairs with my socks on.

At the emergency room, a receptionist, a nurse, a doctor, and then a social worker asked me what happened. Apparently it's standard procedure when confronted with an infant with a broken bone, although I didn't help my cause much by pacing the waiting room, clutching my baby and crying, "I'm so sorry, I'm so sorry, mommy's so sorry."

The fact that it was an accident did not remove the sting of being questioned for hurting my child. And as mother and daughter sat crying in the too bright, sterile hospital room, the doctor very kindly, and very astutely, said, "I promise you, she will never remember this. Unfortunately, you will never forget it."

My daughter came home in a full leg cast, right up to her diaper. It weighed almost as much as she did. But she adjusted quickly, and in fact didn't even seem to notice.

We were supposed to attend a friend's child's birthday party the next day, and that evening my husband said, "You know, if you don't want to go, we don't have to. It might be a little uncomfortable."

"She'll be fine," I said. "The doctor said as soon her leg was set in the cast, it wouldn't hurt anymore."

"Actually," he replied, softly. "I was thinking about you."

I bristled, because I suddenly knew what he meant. Infants with broken bones aren't a common sight.

"It was an accident," I said, finally. "I'm not going to hide for the next month. I didn't do it on purpose. If people ask what happened, I'll tell them. If they don't ask, then they already have an opinion and there's nothing I can do about it. But for God's sake, I can't be the only person this has ever happened to."

And apparently I'm not.

It started at the birthday party. One by one, parents came over to see my baby. It was natural curiosity, and it didn't bother me. What did bother me was the conspiratorial manner in which some of them confessed that they'd had a similar experience.

It continued at the grocery store, the mall, and anywhere else we went. And when I explained what happened, it seemed that some people felt an almost visible relief—relief that they weren't the only ones whose child was a victim of mommy's or daddy's clumsiness, or carelessness, or just plain humanness.

They told me their stories as though sharing a shameful secret. They stepped in a little closer, and in hushed tones said, "When my son/daughter was young, I accidentally . . ." They laughed nervously upon revealing their demon, but I could tell that in most cases, it was somehow cathartic.

I realized then that many truly were sharing a secret. Some of these people had probably never told anyone else the truth about how their kids had gotten hurt, for fear of the social —and legal—consequences. In today's climate of Andrea Yates and pervasive child abuse, it is simply unthinkable to admit to hurting one's child—even without the element of intent.

While I understand the caution, the truth is we're human. We trip, we slip, we fall, we turn away for a moment. I learned the hard way, and I'm sure it won't be my last lesson. I'm not perfect, but I love my children, and I'm a good mother.

And even good mothers make mistakes.

Maggie Lamond Simone

Bringing Home The Bacon

I recently read an article about an English tradition in which a couple is rewarded with a side of bacon for not fighting for a year and a day. I couldn't believe my eyes.

I threw it in front of my husband and cried, "Look at this! We should do it! We should enter the contest! I mean, who couldn't use a side of bacon, right? How hard could it be?"

And I honestly believed it. How difficult could it be to not fight with your spouse? If you loved someone enough to get married, then what could you possibly fight about? Doesn't being married mean that you're always happy? I know my husband is.

So we set up the interview. We were very excited. The contest was ours. It wasn't even fair, really. It was like playing the lottery when you already know the numbers. We sat down with the interviewer, giddy with anticipation.

"Sign us up!" we said. "We want to win a side of bacon! We haven't fought in a year and a day! We're the perfect couple! We're always happy, we don't annoy each other, and neither of us has any irritating habits!"

"Well, wait a second . . ." my husband said slowly, turning to me. "I wouldn't go quite that far. I mean, you know how you never finish a glass of anything? That's kind of irritating."

"Yeah, I guess it is," I replied. "And sometimes, when the bathroom tissue roll is almost empty and I get out a new one and put it on the back of the toilet and you use that instead of finishing up the old one, I guess I get a little annoyed."

"I know, I know," he chuckled. "And how about your concept of punctuality? People may think something's wrong if I'm not five minutes early, but they think the same thing if you're not a half hour late!"

"That is so funny!" I said, laughing. "And so is the way you keep stuffing things into the kitchen garbage as if the bag is going to magically get bigger as time goes on! That cracks me up!"

"No! Stop! You're killing me!" he cried, tears rolling down his cheeks. "Ooh! Ooh! How about the way you order way more than you can eat when we go to a restaurant?! It's like you think you're never going to eat again! That gets me every time!"

Ouch, I thought. It's starting to get a little personal here.

"Oh yeah?" I said, a little hurt. "How do you explain the fact that every time I'm on the telephone, you view it as a prime opportunity to begin a conversation with me? Or your almost inconceivable desire to clean the house before the housekeeper comes?"

"I would say that those are nothing compared to your inexplicable belief that the dishwasher somehow empties itself," he snapped. "And then there's your charming inability to distinguish left from right when giving directions."

"A habit matched in irritability," I shot back, "only by your lack of desire to watch the road."

"I'll tell you what," he replied. "I'll start watching the road more if you'll stop grocery shopping without a list. That 'we need everything' excuse REALLY bothers me."

It was getting ugly. We looked at each other and finally shrugged. None of it mattered. That's not what marriage is about. What matters is that we love each other and our child and try to be good parents and decent people. If we have the occasional argument, it doesn't mean we're not a good couple. It means we're human.

"Hey," he said, putting his arm around me, "Let's get outta here. We don't even like bacon."

Margaret P. Cunningham

The Last Martini at the Bubble Lounge

The whole thing started when my nephew told me he'd gotten a summer job at the Bubble Lounge.
"What on earth is that?" I asked.
"The new martini bar. You haven't been yet?"
"No, I don't believe I have. It's called the Bubble Lounge? Cute name. The last martini at the Bubble Lounge," I said dreamily. "That would be a good title for a short story."
"Uh, yeah. Well, I guess I'd better get going," he said, not certain where the conversation was heading but sure that he didn't want to tag along.
Writing a story to fit a title would horrify Rita, our creative writing instructor at the community college's department of continuing education.
"Build your story around strong characters," she said over and over, "And everything else will follow."
But I couldn't get that title out of my mind. So one evening I drove by the Bubble Lounge. It was the latest addition to the upscale shopping village that had established itself in the heart of our historically significant and recently "discovered" neighborhood. I pictured my neighbors—those endlessly energetic, creative, fixer-upper professionals—behind the bar's frosted glass, sipping elegant concoctions. They would be swapping the latest parenting tidbits, I supposed, or sharing landscaping tips and names of decorators before dashing off to the corner bistro or the gourmet take-out for their dinner.
I pictured it all as I opened a package of pork chops and put potatoes on to boil. And it kept coming back to me. The last martini at the Bubble Lounge. Why the last martini? A story about the closing of a bar? Set in prohibition times? Let it go. But I couldn't. Rita says to start with character. O.K. A tortured soul's final toot before heading off to A.A. It didn't work. Maybe it was more symbolic and personal. In the Bubble Lounge of life, I was, after all, close to the last round.
I thought about it one whole afternoon as I strolled my grandchild past the shops, past the dark lounge that would come alive when dusk settled on the neighborhood. I tried different plots while chatting with some of the nannies in the park across

from my house. I knew I was getting obsessive when I couldn't remember the bid at my bridge group that evening. My mind was not on cards. It was at the Bubble Lounge! I had to write the story and be done with it.

The next day I called my husband Harry at his office.

"I thought you might want to meet me for a drink after work," I suggested as temptingly as possible.

"What's wrong with the back porch?" he said.

"What's wrong with a little change? It would do us good. Then we could grab dinner somewhere."

But the basketball game was on T.V., and he was tired. Another night, maybe.

Two weeks later, "another night" had not materialized. After dinner, I told Harry about my preoccupation with the non-evolving story.

"I don't know what you're talking about. You don't even like martinis," he said and disappeared into his new computer.

I loaded the dishwasher, put on some lipstick and my new black slacks.

"Harry, I'll be back in a little while. I'm going to the Bubble Lounge."

"By yourself?"

"I won't be long."

"Oh, yes. We have drinks other than martinis," said the personable, young bartender who also happened to be my nephew.

So I sat at a tiny corner table by the window, sipping a cosmopolitan—vodka and cranberry juice. Cranberry juice for the bladder and vodka for the soul, I told myself, feeling dramatic. It was served in a martini glass. Soft jazz played, candles flickered, and repartee sparkled—from what I could overhear at the neighboring tables, anyway). It was cozy but cool, everything black and glass and retro or deco. What a treat to spend an hour or so in an environment completely yet so pleasantly alien from one's own. And only a few blocks from home. Home. I thought of Harry, happily lost in the world of the wide web. We had once cherished an evening in a place like this, away from mountains of responsibility and interrupting children, where we could just be together and talk. Our mountains were all relative molehills now. We finally had the time to go whenever and pretty much wherever we wanted. But we were tired. A ballgame on T.V., a good book, a drink with friends on the porch—it was fine, very good, in fact. But no matter how nice the ride, take the same route everyday, and the scenery becomes boring.

"Excuse me." I didn't realize the waiter was standing by me. "A gentleman at the bar would like to know if he may join you."

"Oh, good Lord," I thought and looked toward the bar. Harry lifted his cosmopolitan in salute, pointed to himself and then to me, his eyebrows raised questioningly.

When I stopped laughing, I motioned him over. My nephew stood behind the bar, cleaning a glass and wearing a quizzical smile as he looked from his uncle to me.

"I like this place," said Harry. "Can't believe it's taken us so long to try it out."

He told me about his partner's flaky secretary. It might have been the drinks, but we laughed and laughed. I told him about Rita getting her poetry published. We talked about vacation plans, how we'd like to enlarge the porch, and do some much needed landscaping.

"Last call, folks. Do you want anything else?" said the waiter.

I looked around, and the place was almost empty. Hours had slipped by.

"When was the last time you had a martini?" Harry asked me. Before I could answer, he told the waiter, "Bring the lady a martini."

I watched the young man fill up his tray and serve the other tables. He put the drink in front of me. "There you go," he said. "The last martini at the Bubble Lounge."

Part 3

How far is home?
What place is this?

Night Piece

At 2 a.m. I don't know where I am.
Lamplight circles the room, my book
has fallen to the floor.
Through an open door I see the kitchen
fluorescent, the space heater
pulsing red semaphores over and out.
Why is everything on?

Plucked from sleep, I am still
in the field with the singing horse.
Beyond my window, a hush like snow
defines the continent of night.
One car whines by; a single pair of feet
taps past, hurrying. How far is home?
What place is this?

It was summer in the field: daisies,
early goldenrod. The horse was singing Bach.
Someone said, *We must cut out his heart.*
There were poppies suddenly under the apple trees.
The orchestra went on playing.
The space heater keeps waving red flags.

Does everything imagine itself elsewhere?
Would the horse be here if it could,
keeping warm, while I search for hearts
in long grass?
Is the heater on a dangerous mission?
Whose heart have I lost?
Someone is keeping the true story from me.

– Ann Goldsmith

Some Nights the Dark Hill

When, walking the park at twilight,
I hear footsteps behind me,
I call my silver shepherds, my three
Spirit dogs, and they come,
Padding through the wastes of darkening
Meadow, past the crocodiles in the woods.
Tails low, easy in their stride,
They keep close as they always did,
And the footfalls I thought I heard
Veer aside, onto other paths.

Once, these beasts lolled their blunt heads
Against my thigh, rolled in carrion,
Hunted rabbits and rattlesnakes.
Now I go into the dark with my dogs
And the crocodiles sleep, night simmers,
Black peony on an incense stick.
The frequencies in my spine
Tune to the rustle of silks,
The growls and murmurs under hemlocks.

Some nights, the dark hill of my heart
Shakes out like a rag
And my root system sings electric,
I smell blood on the moon.
Tangled in pink refrains,
I plummet, singing my one lame note,
Down through musk-breathing caverns
To the path by a river veining bone
Where a man my bones know
Walks at evening with his three black dogs.

– Ann Goldsmith

Crossroads

There are no magnolias
on Sulphur Springs Road
    the land is low and silent
    the land is low and still
Only a stop sign dares you
to a state of trespass
Purgatory may be at the end
of that road for all I know
Just never saw a soul
on old Sulphur Springs Road.

– Theresa Wyatt

Best wishes!
Wonderful to
meet you +
hear you read –
9/10/04

Best Shot

She lets go of the moon, strings it out
a swing on ice, it slides into the sky
barren of double-talk
her skirts flow high, she wins the contest
home is the prize

She is the leading character, but no hero
(all sons are prodigal and welcome home)
striving to corner the light
before the sky empties itself
not enough habitat

She fishes with worms at the water hole
enough power from a short arc
to shoot it across to the deepest part
home is the prize
else everything goes in the water

She keeps records on bones
the story of nature's tinkering
barren of double-talk
dry branches hang at odd angles
not enough habitat

Death, that come-from-behind creature
her lonely sibyl
armed with crystal thorns
empties her pockets
everything gone in the water

– Irma Sheppard

Holding Back the Shadows

They lurk,
tap my shoulder and run,
ring my doorbell and disappear
behind laughing trees.
They are remnants
of my mother.
She stitched them into
her housedress pockets,
weighty things
the color of lead.
She passed them along
to me, when I wasn't looking,
too busy to see.
I try to sew them
into words
when I feel them
reaching for the light
in my daughter's eyes.

– Karen Lewis

Funeral Homes

We found out too late
to go to Barb's viewing,

drank tea in a café imagining
the quiet funeral home,
a board with photographs
pasted on, the "director"
discreetly out of sight.
Funeral homes,

yellow lights on the road
between life and death. I run
yellow lights. When I die, please,

no funeral home—read
a few of my poems,
sing "12:30"
by the Mamas and the Papas,
tell a few stories. Eat,
drink.

No heavily carpeted rooms,
no massive doors,
no registry.

If I die in spring, summer, or fall,
a walk in the garden.
If it's winter, chat about
my purple coneflower
or Venus flytrap. Drive home,

remember me when the light
turns green.

– Kenneth Pobo

Things You Do

or leave undone.
A pillowcase not washed
for six months.

The wooden napkin ring,
carved like a gazelle,
empty on the lazy Susan.

Credit card slips
with spiky signatures
still in the desk.

I was never a housekeeper.
How much is mourning,
how much is laziness?

My father's mother left
her husband's pipe on the kitchen mantle
for eight years.

My mother's mother wore black
on her shoulders and in
her dark Irish heart until she died.

Perhaps the old ways were best.
All black for a year,
then touches of gray and lilac.

One certain day it's over,
and all you have is a brooch
with hair in it.

– Gay Baines

Raspberries

The bronze sunset plated
the sky with images
of you,

but if it had been
silver, I could have made
your print

on that cold spring day
when you and I were
in the Berkshires

and you walked down
that mountain
and I was lost,

picking raspberries
and the juices in the basket
bled together like prints,

faded in too much light,
and seeped through
the bands of wood

that were too far apart to help,
like silver nights and bronze sunsets
on Beartown Mountain Road.

– Laura Crews

Grace

Delicate as a lacewing, Grace
admonishes the harsh aspects
of life to take cover, to cower
in her presence.

But the roses' thorns are the
uprising in her garden of soft
purple pansies that hide beneath
the feet of yellow irises, small
orbiting suns in the pansies'
way of thinking.

Grace's thorn-blood covers her
garden's innocence with an
uninvited ruddiness, the malignant
spots on plants just measles in
Grace's mind, badness a disease
that always runs its course in
due time.

Most think Grace's eyes, the
color of lingcod, are cold as ice,
fleshed out for now, but doomed
to melt within her face born from
the girth of evil within innocence.

– Claire T. Feild

How night comes on in January

one minute you look up
it's the five o'clock
dregs of a January day
ten minutes later
the light's sucked out
of an old man's mouth.
He's emptied his cup
turned it upside down
in the saucer.

– Sandra Cookson

All Day I Have Been Afraid

I heard Mrs. Lee scream *Kill me! Kill me!*
from inside her house and I did not move.

At noon, all the dogs in the neighborhood
began barking wildly. Was an unbearable truth

being told in a pitch that only they could hear?
The television said E. coli is lurking

in my laundry and kitchen sponge, and toxic
waste is being dumped into drinking water.

A bright disc with many lights hovered
in the afternoon sky above the backyard fence.

A small child came to my door and asked
if I wanted to buy a chance—*Yes! More chances!*

I said, and took twenty. The sun, my once
cheerful companion, grips the hills and lowers herself

like a dying woman easing into her sickbed.
The August wind, quiet, slowly prowls

through the rooms. Bats begin to swoop nooses
over my head. Now

the sharp moon appears, a bright machete
swung high above me in the evening sky.

– Jeff Walt

The Red in Cold Breath

Autumn has lumbered its last few steps into winter,
breathless up a hill and careless down with soldiers' counts
of hours and minutes survived, a cadence to dull events
endured with the breath of agonies holding to their necks.

Time is a play actor with mask and costume of night,
a parody of the easy passing of dark over the next loss.

Questions whisper while there are no mikes or cameras,
just as they whisper at home during the deadly wait.
"What did the first shot have that needs to go on and on?
"Why is that patience that ran out on talk sought now for deaths?"

We should have known that words suffer their treasons.
What was once the danger in fact has become a chance
for the possibilities of threats to us all.

So this winter's cold and dark are numb under siege.
Seasons suffer damage, but war loses because it began.

– Michael Tritto

Harvard Square on Christmas Eve

—for Louisa Solano and the people of Grolier Poetry Book Shop

The door cracks wide and deep
as I dive headfirst into the venerable
bookstore seeking shelter from the slant-
wise rain. Inside the escape hatch I breathe
at last, yet words like water choke
and I gasp for air. Across this aquarium
the owner throws a lifeline and fish food
to a novice learning to swim.

How can I help? she asks
for she sees not simply a customer
but a would-be, may-be poet
casting a net. She fields questions,
proffers wisdom, lends an ear
to the word emerging in the
modest manger of my life.
After long minutes listening
to a litany she must have heard
rehearsed a thousand times,
she drops a depth charge, breaking the news.
In a bush-whacked economy,
a world averse to verse
and awash in war, the well has run dry.
The doors will close, barring a miracle.

Quietly we return to our business:
shopping and shelving,
browsing and bailing out the flood.
I buy two books, fumble for feeble words
to convey gratitude or hope.
The door closes behind me.

Outside, the homeless tin man
greets me, his sign reporting AIDS
abruptly, like a worn medical chart.

Dreadlocks fly as the sea lion roars
and holiday shoppers indulge their
impulse-buying instincts in megastores,
smiles frozen like creatures of the deep.

Rain falls, and the young man playing guitar
hopes that lightning will strike, for once.
The national security code flashes bright orange,
an empty beacon in this Christmas storm of scarlet
and green.

A homeless carnival barker peddles *Spare Change News*.
Hey young man!
Have a heart
        Haveaheart
                Haveaheart
                        Haveaheart.

Christmas eve at the bottom of the sea.

                        – *Alexander Levering Kern*

Hosing Down Cows

The granite rock ran out of water to steam in the Sun.
Everyone is afraid of campfires.
Farmers are hosing their cows
to keep them from dropping, but still
many fall to the side,
their legs point to the sky
and beg for peace with longer shadows
in early afternoons.
New predators in mute cells of dead birds
prepare to be born again,
to join the armies
out of the remains of their kin.
Even the Sun has turned
from the outstretched arms
of the disturbed Earth
crowded with the knowledge of winter.

– Gabor Kovacsi

"A Night of Yelling Couldn't Coax Cows Out of Deadly Barn"
–Cooperstown News Bureau, NY

Schoharie Creek couldn't hold.
Four feet of snow melted in as many hours.
Riffles turned to cascades, cross logs to weirs,
a churning damnation
of red clay burst its banks.

It was the ark gone wrong.
He felt it when he entered the barn,
puppies floating, calves knee deep
in wet straw. Then it was waist deep;
he got what he could to the loft,
nine puppies, eight calves, the dog.

The horses knew enough to run
for higher ground, but cows,
right for milking, scared dumb,
stayed where they thought safety was.

He sang to them all night,
calling each cow by name,
to let a voice they trusted
startle them past drowning, hypothermia.
There were curses late when his herd
was dying, a horror of white eyes
shaking a wooden cavern to blindness;
and all that goddamned bellowing, gurgling,
"Sweet Jesus, save my heart from this."

Sixty-nine milkers dead in the morning,
a few survivors stood on their corpses.
A sanity shared by the tenderness of puppies,
the hunger of calves kept his hands busy,
a mercy denied Job.

– Bill Brown

Darkly, Darkly, If At All

My husband tells our son his generation
Doesn't deserve his father's, and he leaves.
My son asks if this is true.

In the window of the old library, where
No one goes, I spent the afternoon
Reading some Russian poets.

It is a broad sill, you have to
Climb a bit to get up. I was a child again.
One doesn't unsay things, of course,

To children, but one thinks:
No one deserves anyone really.
Yet we have us. I am reading

Anna Akhmatova who lost so much, and seeing
The photo we all know of the ecstatic girl
Kissing her soldier, the war over.

Would I willingly give up my children
To even a just war. Would I say,
OK, finally, for the common good,

Or because God told me to,
Like Abraham. Would I not say, even then,
Get on the train to Canada, maybe He

Won't see you. And yet here is
Anna Akhmatova, 1889-1966. "It is not
Permitted me to take away anything."

– Janet McCann

Hansel Writes to Gretel
From the House of Madness

Gretel,

I left the home of our parents before sunrise,
while you were still sleeping in the trundle-bed upstairs,
and set out on my own through the coastal redwoods.

Droplets of water fell from the trees
soaking the ferns and rotting logs on the forest floor.
My cap and vest and boots got wet clean through.

Remembering past experiences, I carried no breadcrumbs,
dropping thoughts on the path instead, hundreds of them.
A hermit thrush with a reddish tail ate every one of them.

By mid-afternoon, I'd found the hut again,
its walls constructed of yellow pimpernel,
its roof of fringed loosestrife. You remember.

I carried the agate for protection just as before.
It gave me no protection. Just as before.
The interior of the hut burned greenly. As before.

This time Fox Spirit was there, crouching
in front of the great oven, mouth of stars,
paws of cloud, eyes of rain, teeth of flame.

He asked me to enter his mind
through the edge of a mirror he held up
in front of my face. I did as he asked.

I wish you were here now, peering
in at me through the grate. Till you arrive,
I remain, roasting slowly on my bed of coals,

                              Your Loving Brother, Hansel

                                        – John Gilgun

Immolation Dress

My dress is made of war and hunger,
tattoos from the wrists of refugees,
audio clips from the evening news,
ink from the rebel song.
Who is watching?
My eyes are made of fire.
I am not afraid to be the lamb.
Can a voice inside a flower
be made of such violence?
Would the world stand still
as I make myself a dress
made of paper and fire?
Write a news story out of this:
the immolation will bear red fruit
on the fruit seller's stand.
Where there are hungry mothers
there will be a god making soup.
Where there are wounded men
there will be a god knitting bandages.
I want to know who walks the world
without hunger, I want to know who
is not hungry who walks this world
with feet made of clouds, praising.

– Ava Hu

Placards

I'm jealous.
Unbelievable. Chaos
creates heroes & martyrs.
I'm neither, & want it.

Why can't I carry a sign
with a photograph from 1985,
& say to the camera,
This is my husband.

His name is Ted.
He's five-eight,
with English blue eyes,
wearing a leather jacket,

an olive beret. If you
see him, send him back.
Tell him I love him
& want to find him.

The day he died
tumbles back in time,
taking him further & further
away from me.

I see him from behind,
or across the playing field,
but it's never Ted, just
a doppelganger. I look at

the split meadow, crashed offices,
the towers burning,
& wonder what I did wrong,
stupid as Lot's wife.

– Gay Baines

Tell Me

"Tell me about your father."
His clear blue eyes are steady, measured.
                              He waits.
This tall man who intimidated me
when I stood on defiant legs next to his
                              tall son.
He is broken by the disease and a
wife who soon will not
                    know him.
I want to say lightly, "What about my father?"
But his eyes hold mine.
                    I know.
I know what he is asking and I tell him
about my father who was
                    eaten
by the same monster that lurks in him.
I tell him there was no
                    pain.
"The pills and shots," I say. "He faded. He slept
in his chair and then his bed, and then he
                    was gone."

I am finished.

                    He waits.

"Sometimes he was anxious," I say. I cannot say
"afraid." Fathers are not
                    afraid.
"There were pills. I don't know what they were.
They helped."
                    He nods.
His face is impassive. "Will you find out?"
he asks softly.
                    I nod.

                                        – *Lorraine Jeffery*

August 18, 1587

Virginia Dare, first child born in the new country. Her
grandfather went back to England to get help, came back
3 years later but there was no sign of any of them

In that fall, as leaves went
blood with her child squalling
her mother must have clawed
wisteria, dreamt of orange trees
loaded with fruit as ice crept
into buckets and the dark came
too fast. No one knows if the
corn faltered, the flood bank
rose. No one knows if a roof
collapsed, bones broke, if men
crept in with hatchets, the baby
in her arms as snow piled higher
than the chinked window. The
mother might have torn the dress
she wore for teas in Essex into
swaths to soothe her child's
burning skin, or to make a doll's
dress for the corn cob figure her
child giggled and cried to have
near her bed. Were there gaps
in her memory, going over the
smell of English roses, the weather,
the porcelain cups for tea. She
could load the gun but would
she use it on a stranger in the
middle of the night with the baby
between them. Did she hold it in
her hands as if it were another's
fingers as the moon slithered thru
burlap and the rough weave never
let her forget where she was

– *Lyn Lifshin*

Autumn

> ...more alive than anywhere else in the world.
> —Lorca

The last flung-back, bullet-struck
moment of the Republican soldier
on an arid Andalusian slope

> of the Spanish Civil War,
> his death framed by Robert Capra,
> that came to frame a century of war,
> his body halfway falling back

in another country, forever toward
his shadow, his rifle pointed at heaven,
his head turned away, forgetting the way back.

> The woman's gaunt stare
> skyward, her grimaced lips drawn back
> from her teeth, forehead deeply
> plowed with wrinkles,

her eyes straining
to find the flying sewing-machine,
stitching clouds

> with threads of fear.
> What happened? The dusty
> dive-bombed rubble of Barcelona,

the child at the slope of her breast
nursing on oblivion, the arbored
boulevards lost in explosions of leaves.

– Walter Bargen

Kandace Brill Lombart

Les Mots d'Amour

For years, the rabbits had been romping, performing their dance of courtship in my backyard. For years, I enjoyed their presence, marveling at their activity, laughing at their leaps.

A dead December rabbit is below my writing window. Ravenous crows are eyeing their dinner from above, waiting to disembowel the supine corpse under my sight. I had to bury it, cover it, something, but I couldn't. So I asked my neighbor if he had the stomach to pick it up for me. He couldn't either, perhaps for the same reasons as mine. He queried, "Have you ever eaten rabbit?" Little did he know how many times I had walked to market while living in France to pluck a fresh rabbit off the *marché* butcher's rack for the evening stew. I left it to simmer for long hours in red wine, raisins, shallots and bacon; or another recipe (one of my husband's favorites) was *lapin à la moutarde*, a dish basted in Dijon mustard to thicken the sauce.

I returned to the keyboard, the animal's carcass stretched before me under the windowsill before the computer screen. My stomach made its own twists and turns as my memory returned to our family meals around a small, white, round table, in a small French kitchen with two bay windows and fluffy, diaphanous checkered orange and white curtains, next to a noisy highway. When I served my three lively children and teasing husband a *gourmand* lover's rabbit stew, he pretended to "suck" the eyes out of the rabbit's head to provoke the children's shrieks in shock: *"Ugh, Papa!"*

It has been at least twenty-one years since I made that recipe.

He would recite his own story of his pet rabbit he kept during the war. Rations were low and the family was hungry for meat; the only thing left to eat was the rabbit.

Even though he was just a child in Belgium during the war, he refused to let anyone kill his cherished pet but himself. Would his older brother remember that story? I must write to him so that he can recite his version to my oldest daughter, who will be at their Christmas dinner table.

And yet another moment around a rabbit: my brother's Christmas gift to my three-year-old daughter when we lived in St.

Germain-en-Laye, the place where we were so happy; the suburb where I could never be happy as a young widow with our children. The gray, puppet-like, stuffed rabbit was still in our basement, somewhere here in America. Dirty and mildewed though it was, I could not toss it out.

Suddenly, all those memories around a rabbit, rabbits, the rabbit, from that rabbit out there. *Le lapin mort.*

I decided to face the responsibility. (It couldn't be any worse than seeing his neck, all those years ago, in the hospital's basement where they wheeled him into a "special" room. He had that silly smile on his face.) So I gathered some newspapers and a small box. At first, I intended only to cover the once-living thing respectfully, place the box over it, and wait for someone else to pick it up. But not let the crows devour it. How long had it been dead? What predator left this animal at my windowsill and didn't have hunger pangs for its innards? Was my cat the culprit? Or was I responsible when I swept some birdseed outside the garage door the other day, intending to leave it for the squirrels. Perhaps that little rabbit . . . *mon petit lapin.*

How could a dead rabbit, just before Christmas, a symbol of an offering, a metaphor for so many memories, be there for me to witness? I could write another tale, another fable, another short-short story entitled: "The Widow and the Rabbit."

As I covered it with newspapers, I simply lifted it, enveloped it with a prayer, and laid it gently in the box, then took it to the curb for the weekly garbage pickup. And that was it.

Until this . . . I can't stop writing about rabbits, my memories of the rabbit and him. *Le lapin mort dans mon jardin aujourd'hui . . . son cou cassé, comme un coup de lapin.*

One summer morning, a Simca-Chrysler car barreled out of the elite residences from the "Golf de Fourqueux" onto the French National highway 307 that elongated the Marly Forest and bordered the Parisian suburban town of St. Germain-en-Laye. It soared up the slope behind the cyclist who was in his glory climbing higher, always higher, effortlessly, airily, pushing himself on each successive ride as if he were training for a bicycling veteran's cross-country marathon. He was positioned straight on the highway, returning home to close the window in the bedroom and finish his strawberries for breakfast. The wife and children were vacationing in Belgium. The car plowed right into the cyclist. He did not feel a thing (she hoped); he was catapulted twenty yards, landed face down on the edge of the ditch. The custom-made bicycle went flying in the air, the back wheel bent, as if someone had taken a slice of metal pie from its frame. He had hardly a scratch.

His neck cracked clean as a whistle; he lay in the ditch, anonymous for days in the morgue; no one knew who the bicyclist was. He taunted his lively children, as he sucked the eyes out of the rabbit his wife prepared so lovingly, all those years ago . . . *mon petit lapin,* she sang, *mon petit lapin de Corentin* . . . .

Perfect

We walked a path of pine needles,
bronzed by the mist, from his house
to the Grand River. Nothing was so quiet
as the boat drifted on slow water. We made
no effort. Sky and clouds lay at the gunwales,
and herons lifted with wisps of morning fog
as we drew near. I told him the dream
I had years before in which he left by a plane
that taxied close to our boyhood home;
I watched him board and fly away.

In his last days he lies in the bed,
needed things near, and tells me
that colors—he tries to describe them
and can't say if he dreams—pool deeply
around him. *They are perfect*, he says.
They buoy him among walls, clock,
bedside table, and curtain as I lean
to kiss him and leave the room.

– James Sedwick

Snow in Leningrad

1.

Blizzard here in Washington, I'm shoveling snow.
My mind sifts snow in Leningrad, World War Two, the Siege,
as I try to track my Aunt Maria . . . She steps over snowy ruins

and people dead of famine, illness, shells. Bless early dusk and snows
that mask the dead a while. No burials till the hard ground thaws.
She lugs rubble from wrecked buildings to raise new barracks.

Nights, she mans an anti-aircraft gun. One wretched crust a day.
Bombs hit her flat, in Pushkin's former stables, but a captain rescues her,
says, "Come, teach English to our officers: someday they'll need it."

At headquarters she gets a cup of soup with bread, a place to sleep,
safer if not warm but no one is. Medals afterwards. She survives
the war, more blizzards, tribulations from the KGB.

They allow her to teach English, French, and keep her piano.
She moves into three barrack rooms in a village north of Leningrad.
She dares not write, but sends me picture books.

2.

A luminous June, 1986. At last we meet. Eighty-one, half-blind,
she serves me tea and tells of childhood skating on the Neva,
troika rides across St. Petersburg, walks with Akhmatova and Blok,

those nine hundred nights the Germans ringed the wounded town.
Her champion Airedale disappeared for someone's cooking pot.
Now a small white mutt and large gray cat sleep on her feet:

Trust creatures more than certain humans . . .
But Ludmilla, her neighbor, is faithful, discreet.
December 1991. Ludmilla writes:

Maria's gone to hospital. Midnights she wakes
the ward with lectures on Pushkin, Bach,
Dickens, English grammar, and Voltaire.

3.

My plane from Washington lands a day too late.
By three metros and a bus Ludmilla takes me miles
across the city heaped with dirty snow. No neighborhoods

for foreigners. We skirt the hospital on snowy paths
that lead us to the morgue. A white-smocked worker chases out
a dappled cat who slips back in, resumes his watch beside the slab

where my chilled aunt lies in state. She wears her blue professor dress,
beret she swore she would wear to the grave . . . Through falling snow
we escort her to the marble crematorium. Friends flock.

Something like a service. Then the fire—the Church forbids it but
she'd seen too many dead awaiting spring. Attendants, thrifty, saved
the clothes. The coffin slides through low brass doors.

We troop to her old flat, repaired, and toast her soul's
lone journey through the snowy skies. The rest will go
beneath a churchyard stone.

4.

Washington, 2002. In this wind swirling white
I seek her still, and still the night is blind. My attempts to fix
her life in words freeze, then melt with flakes of snow.

Yet, as if these were the drifts that cloak
the stone above her distant sack of ash,
I keep on shoveling.

– Elisavietta Ritchie

Bill Glose

Collateral Damage

Collateral Damage. When mentioned casually, it sounds antiseptic, like a term from biology class—clinical and guiltless. But sitting in my recliner and watching the war in Iraq, I remember a time when I was more than just a spectator, and I feel anything but guiltless.

In February of 1991, I was a rifle platoon leader in the 82nd Airborne Division, awaiting orders for the invasion of Iraq. My platoon was positioned along the tri-border area between Iraq, Kuwait, and Saudi Arabia. We were weary from months of preparation in 120-degree heat, with only a monthly shower for hygiene and plastic-encased MRE's for sustenance. Pulpy flakes shed from our scalps, sand coated every inch of our skin, and blasts from thousand-pound bombs echoed across the border, reverberating through our bones. When we received the orders to begin the ground phase of The Gulf War, we wondered what it would be like to plunge into territory we'd been bombing for a month, what the explosions would feel like up close. News estimates forecasted up to 45,000 American casualties, and we furtively glanced amongst ourselves, wondering which ones would not return, and quietly praying it wasn't us.

On February 24, we crossed into Iraq. We raced through the desert, finding scattered destruction, unexploded bombs, and deserted hideouts. As armored columns raced ahead, Republican Guard Forces retreated, surrendered, or were destroyed. We chased the battle, clearing bypassed bunker complexes and abandoned war facilities, performing a *movement to contact* whenever enemy forces were suspected. *Movement to Contact* was another clinical term used in the business of killing. Arrows drawn on maps detailed our planned route and suspected enemy positions, but movement on the ground was more complex than the grease pencil lines suggested. Sometimes we found signs of mutiny—bloated, uniformed bodies with small caliber wounds to the head—and other times we discovered soldiers left behind. Some fought but most surrendered, obeying the few Arabic phrases we'd been taught phonetically: *Da-a-si-LAHK ala-as-FAL* (Put your weapon down)! *Kha-LI id-ik ala al-AA* (Keep your hands up)!

Complicating our task was the fact that soldiers were discarding uniforms to blend in with the population. We treated everyone as a potential threat until they were searched, interrogated, and separated from their weapons. In searching a prisoner, one soldier pointed an M-16 at him while another frisked him. With language barriers and years of dictatorial justice, captives often misunderstood our intent. While we were searching a family we had found rooting through an abandoned ammunition depot, the children openly cried and pled for their lives, thinking we were about to execute them. When we finished, patted them on their backs and handed them spare MRE's, the surprise in their faces was enough to make the months in the desert worth it for me.

Using our translator, they volunteered to join our battle against Saddam. They yelled the few phrases of English they knew—*George Bush, America Number One,* and *Big Mac*—coupling each with a thumbs-up gesture. One boy showed off a relatively new pair of Nike sneakers he had somehow obtained, delighted with his own little piece of Americana—an oddity in this land of sandals. Driving away in a dilapidated truck, they continued cheering while I stood in their wake, amazed at their resilience, and feeling rather pleased for my part in their liberation.

The next day Hussein surrendered unconditionally. The war was over, but we kept up our guard. We cast keen eyes at the sand, wary of unexploded CBU's. Cluster Bomb Units littered the countryside, delivered by aircraft capable of carrying *30,000* of the bomblets on a single mission. Ironically, our greatest threat came from our own munitions.

One of our patrols ran across several burned-out vehicles. Most were military, but one was a simple truck that had run over a CBU. Men gawked at the twisted metal and the scorched remains of the passengers, but I turned my focus elsewhere. Alongside the damaged truck, one item caught my eye. I picked it up and turned it over in my hands. It was fairly new, but tattered nonetheless from an explosion I had never even heard. The swoosh of the Nike logo shown to me with pride just days before was now barely recognizable. As I fingered the torn shoe, I remembered the energetic cheers of children happy to be alive, praising us as saviors.

Swallowing hard, I no longer felt pleased with myself. I

rationalized that we hadn't started this war, that we were simply responding to unprovoked aggression, and that collateral damage was a fact of war. None of that made me feel any better though, and none of that would help the poor kid who had simply stepped in the wrong place at the wrong time. The child may have been a citizen of the country we were fighting, but he was one of the oppressed we were trying to save as well.

In war, I know collateral damage will happen. The term may sound clinical while watching CNN videos of a country half-a-world away, numbers scrolling on the screen to account for civilian casualties. But for me, the term will always bring to mind grimmer realities of war. And a tiny sneaker. And one wrong step.

Part 4

*Grab a handful from your basket
of hopes and clothespins*

Garden Song

Millions died to make this loam,
to tint this cloud, to feed this leaf.
Mayflies, magpies, wasps and goats—
down went their bodies from the air
to give us this, this perfect day.

This is the day for which the night
filled itself with shattered stuff
and dampness slid from spot to spot
and eyes were hatched to see the sky,
to give us this, this perfect day.

Praise, and curse, this perfect day.

– Sally A. Fiedler

Red Tail

Years ago driving west,
Indiana back to Illinois,
I was taking in the late-day slant
of sunlight, color of bourbon,
on fields of beans and corn.
Here and there a combine
trailing a cloud of chaff
chugged along like a lonely ship.
On a fencepost I saw a hawk
looking toward the Interstate,
looking directly my way.
A few days later I started working
on this poem. In the first versions
I had the hawk speak human words
for the endless prairie that once was,
before being plowed into nothing;
an elegy for the black soil broken,
sprayed and injected
with fertilizers and poison,
laid bare to the wind all winter.
But what I left out was the mellow,
lovely whiskey of the light,
and the browns and yellows
of stalks, husks, leaves and stems.
I left out the tireless solitude
of each farmer inside each combine—
back and forth all day
like a poet on the lonely page.
I left out the gorgeous solitude of that hawk
perched and motionless on a bare fencepost,
and—of course—my own solitude
bathed in that glowing, yellow last-light
like the cheeks and forearms of the farmers,
like the speckled breast feathers of the hawk,
like the endless fields giving up the harvest.

                                         – *Matthew Murrey*

Mary Ann Eichelberger

The Letter Writer

Every Sunday after lunch Julia wrote letters.

Once, like many New Yorkers residing on the Upper East Side, she and her mother devoted Sunday afternoons to making social calls, to receiving visitors, or in cultural pursuits. One bleak, wet Sunday, when she was in her early forties, the prospect of venturing forth alone in raincoat and rubbers, toting an umbrella, was unappealing. She had seen all the current exhibits at the Metropolitan Museum, Carnegie Hall was closed, and she owed no one a visit and expected no one to call. The old-fashioned custom of paying calls on a Sunday afternoon was no longer observed by any but the very oldest of her mother's acquaintances and they had been dying off at an alarming rate.

On that dismal afternoon, Julia stood at the window watching the scurrying pedestrians and shuddered at the thought of leaving the cozy apartment, but if she did not go out, what would she do with herself all afternoon? After early morning services with her mother she had read *The New York Times*. She might have liked to attempt the crossword puzzle, but that had always been her mother's challenge.

She felt she must make a quick decision before her mother propelled her out into the rain by the sheer force of her expectations that her daughter would venture forth as she did every Sunday afternoon. She must have a solid reason for deviating from the norm. The fact that it was a nasty day would not mollify her mother who did not tolerate changes in established patterns.

She squeezed her eyes shut, thinking hard, listening to the cold rain sluicing down the window. Happily, she remembered the note on a former classmate's Christmas card. Actually, it was two lines beneath the signature: "Hope all is well with you and your mother. If ever I'm in town perhaps we could do lunch."

Julia and her mother read many meanings into that message from the friend (who now lived in Texas), deciding it would be exciting to see her again. They led such a monotonous life, any diversion was welcome.

Now Julia said, "I am ashamed to admit I never answered the note on Felicia's Christmas card. I wonder if I should do that instead of going out this afternoon? It really is rude of me to keep putting it off."

A stickler for good manners, her mother agreed. "Yes, I think you should do that. You wouldn't want Felicia to think you didn't care."

Relieved, Julia said, "I could use that lovely note paper Dwight gave me for Christmas. With the border of roses."

Her mother (who always did the *Times* crossword puzzle in ink) suspended her Parker pen over the paper and nodded approval. "But do not use one of those dreadful ballpoint pens. You cannot do justice to your penmanship with a pen like that. You always had good penmanship. When you were at Miss Hale's all your teachers remarked about your good penmanship. And posture. You always had good posture. I credit Miss Hale with that, she never tolerated slumping in her pupils. All her pupils grew up with good posture and excellent penmanship. You may use my other Parker, the black one. It's in the desk drawer where you'll also find a bottle of blue ink."

An hour passed before Julia sat down at the Chippendale desk. First there was a discussion between the two women over what to write. It was agreed that the tone of the letter should be cordial, but not eager. It wouldn't do to sound as if she had nothing better to do, true as it was, than to anticipate a luncheon date with a school friend she hadn't seen in twenty years. After they agreed on the contents of the letter, they rejected the rosebud-bordered notepaper. Every box of stationery her brother had ever given her for Christmas was critically examined until a pale blue with a darker border was selected.

Her mother put aside the crossword puzzle and retired to her room for her afternoon nap. Julia, sitting with perfect posture at the desk, had a sudden inspiration. She could write letters every Sunday instead of paying calls on old ladies or going to concerts that made her nod off or, in nice weather, feeding the pigeons in Central Park until it was time to go home.

A new routine was established. Every Sunday after lunch she wrote letters. It took her hours to compose a single page, so meticulous was she over every word. She wrote detailed notes on all her Christmas cards. Immediately after the New Year she occupied herself answering every little note on the Christmas cards she received, although it was puzzling that fewer and fewer wrote messages as the years went by. The number of cards received also dwindled.

Julia was employed as a reader for a publishing house, a job that was supposed to be temporary when she first graduated from Sarah Lawrence. She never aspired to become an editor or to rise through the ranks to any other position. Coming from an old New York family, she and her parents assumed she would one day make a "good" marriage. They never admitted that she had become one of life's unclaimed treasures. Her job was acquired through her father's connections and she was the longest-lasting reader they ever had. She refused to read manuscripts that contained "sex," murmuring that such books were not "her taste." In deference to her, or more probably to the lingering power of her late millionaire father, she was assigned historical novels and biographies of distinguished clergymen and their ilk. She was tolerated, never controversial, but dismissed as eccentric by her co-workers. It was known that she lived in a large apartment on Fifth Avenue and came to work in a taxi. This set her apart from the ordinary working girls who rattled their way to work on the subway, clutching their purses and brown paper bags containing bologna sandwiches.

Over the years her meager supply of friends shrank along with the Christmas cards so that her main social outlet became the writing of letters. Every Sunday she wrote to her brother, but Dwight never replied except with infrequent telephone calls. She also wrote once a month to her nephew and niece, although they never replied, except with an occasional Hallmark card that said "Thinking of You." It never occurred to her that her letters were unread after they were opened and shaken out in hopes of a check flying out.

She longed for dependable correspondents. It was this longing that brought about her adventure into "pen pals." At first she was leery, but succumbed when her mother suggested a post office box, thus protecting her from the possibility of being confronted by an "undesirable."

It was thrilling to find letters in the box. She and her mother chose the correspondents from lists in the *Saturday Review Of Literature*. Suddenly their lives were full of the doings of others. It became impossible to remain organized without the purchase of a file cabinet to keep all the letters in individual folders.

Hester, the housekeeper, complained that the file cabinet

was ugly next to the antique desk, that it was too heavy to move and that it was ruining the Persian rug. What did Julia care? Every day she hurried to the post office on her way home from work and, heart beating expectantly, clutched envelopes with different postmarks to read after dinner. Hester grumbled that mother and daughter were becoming indifferent to what they ate. Once the two women had observed the amenities of fine dining, from the clear broth through the fish course and the roast to the silver finger bowls floating thin slices of lemon. Now they skipped the soup and fish, concentrated on the main course, salad and dessert, and rushed into the living room with their coffee to peruse the letters.

The letter writing took up so much of Julia's time that she began to begrudge the time she spent at work. It was decided she should quit her job. She certainly did not need the money. At the same time Hester "packed it in" because of "aching joints" and a feeling that her efforts were no longer appreciated by the correspondence-crazed women.

It was inevitable that most of the original pen pals fell by the wayside, but one, Leonard Bixby, remained faithful. Through his letters Julia and her mother learned that he lived with his older sister in a big old house off Grand River in Detroit. His occupation was respectable. He was a vice-president of the Bank of Detroit, in the mortgage department. He frequently told of the problems of fluctuating interest rates and Julia commiserated with him in her replies. When his sister suffered a stroke he wrote of the burden of her care, the irresponsibility of the nurses, the lack of dependable household help. Julia daringly alluded to her willingness to help out, if only she lived closer.

His detailed reply to that generous offer was signed Fondly, Len.

Julia and her mother concluded that he was a sensitive, appreciative man. They sent his sister two Barbara Pym novels, *Excellent Women* and *A Glass Of Blessings* and were rewarded with a long, grateful letter from Len.

Many hours were spent speculating about his looks, but they never dared suggest he send a photograph. That would be bold. His weekly letter, which ran seven to eight pages, arrived every Friday, giving them ample time to pore over every word before Julia penned her reply on Sunday afternoon.

Most of the other pen pals became unimportant and

eventually faded into oblivion. However, every letter she had ever received was kept in the ugly steel file cabinet.

Dwight was intrigued with the file cabinet when he came for his annual visits, but since his sister kept it locked he had no idea what was kept in it and he could not badger her into revealing its contents. He concentrated his energy convincing the two women that they had allowed their haphazard housekeeping to make a mess of their once immaculate apartment. The maid who trudged through the rooms every day did little more than rearrange the dust and take the garbage out while she was plugged into her Walkman. The garbage, Dwight noted, was mostly boxes and trays from Stouffer's and Swanson's Frozen Dinners. He insisted that they could not go on living that way, compromising their standards. "What do you think Father would say about this?" he demanded. He hired a housekeeper who attacked the bathrooms and kitchen with Lysol and made the dust bunnies scurry.

Julia's mother died in her sleep one afternoon while the housekeeper vacuumed under her bed.

Now Julia was all alone, the only bright spot in her life the weekly letter from Len.

Len's sister died in the ambulance on the way to the hospital after he found her gasping for air before breakfast one morning.

Now Len was all alone with nothing to look forward to except his weekly letter from Julia.

She tried not to dwell on her loneliness. Weeks went by when the only conversations she had were with the housekeeper, the doorman and cab drivers. Her brother stopped phoning after he could not persuade her to give up the large apartment and rent a smaller one. She was astute enough to realize Dwight was more interested in conserving the bulk of their parents' estate for himself than he was in his sister's comfort. Her lawyer assured her she would never run out of funds.

It was comforting.

Len's letters were comforting, also. Until he wrote of his plans to visit New York to check on the stock exchange and mortgage departments at various banks. He was retiring soon, but he liked to keep his hand in things.

Finally he set a date for his arrival. The thought of Len being in the same city gave Julia palpitations. When he wrote asking if they might meet she burst into tears because her mother was dead and there was no one for her to turn to for advice.

She didn't write her Sunday letter to Len.

She could not keep away from her post office box the following Friday, where, trembling, she found a letter from the ever faithful Len. With a mixture of fear and joy she read that he was sorry his suggestion that they meet upset her. He knew her so well through the years of correspondence that this could be the only reason why she had not written as usual.

Encouraged by his sensitivity, Julia replied, delicately alluding to the fact that although it seemed as if they knew one another, they had never been properly introduced. But when she dropped the letter into the mailbox she had the eerie sensation that those were her mother's words, not hers. Walking slowly home she realized with a shock that she was still living by her mother's rules, still afraid to meet her disapproval. She wondered if she had ever had any original thoughts or words of her own.

Len responded with the suggestion that she name a public place where they could meet. He confessed that he had often dreamed of meeting her, but, until now, had never dared to hope it could be possible. He promised that as a gentleman he would never press her to reveal her address, that he would not compromise her in any way.

All alone with her emotions, Julia almost, but not quite, admitted to herself that she had frequently fantasized about coming face to face with Len, but even in her wildest imaginings had never thought it could ever happen. Romantic things like that were for other women. Now she asked herself, what was wrong with Len's plan? She did not allow her mother's face or stern voice to rise from the grave.

She wrote to Len on Saturday, which was enough of a disruption of her routine to give her confidence in her ability to make decisions for herself. She chose a restaurant for their meeting that was two blocks from her apartment, one she occasionally visited for lunch, one of the very few restaurants in the neighborhood that had not changed hands in recent years. Being in familiar surroundings would certainly make her more comfortable.

The morning of the meeting, a Monday, she dressed carefully in a navy blue suit, a purchase she had made the previous week after inspecting her closet and realizing that she had bought nothing new since her mother had died. Thinking of her mother gave her a little twitch of anxiety. What would her mother think of her now? Firmly, she put her mother out of her mind.

When she was ready, she inspected herself in a full-length mirror. Her hair, she was shocked to see, was more gray than brown, her eyes a faded blue behind pink rimmed glasses. How long, she wondered in amazement, had it been since she had actually looked at herself?

Her knees trembled and she collapsed on the edge of a Louis IV chair clutching her Coach bag in her hands, her heart sinking rapidly. What had she been thinking when she agreed to Len's invitation? He would find the woman in the flesh was not the romantic correspondent he had known through the years. Would she find him a disappointment, too? Until now everything between them had been safely on paper, their imaginations could make them anything they wanted to be to one another. That was more real to her than the prospect of coming face to face with him, to have him unmasked before her just as she would be unmasked before him. She had never been involved in an intimate relationship. Her relationship with her mother had been a carefully staged affair, a study in good manners and appropriate behavior. Feelings had always been kept in close check. It was, after all, vulgar to give in to one's emotions.

The china clock on the mantel chimed once, reminding Julia that Len planned to arrive at the restaurant at one o'clock. He wrote that he would wear a navy blue suit, a white shirt and a maroon and blue striped tie. In his buttonhole would be a white rosebud and he would carry a companion white rosebud for her. It was by the rosebuds, he wrote, that she would recognize him.

She stood up and once more scrutinized her image in the mirror. She admired the new suit, the white silk blouse, the double strand of cultured pearls clasped around her neck. Then finger by finger she smoothed on navy kid gloves and panicked, thinking that maybe Len should have been content with what had brought them so much happiness in the past, their letters. Perhaps she would not keep their appointment.

But she had promised to meet him at a quarter past one and a lady always keeps a promise.

She left her apartment and walked briskly to the restaurant.

He was seated at a table near the window. Julia recognized him, not by the rosebud in his lapel, but because he was exactly the way she had imagined, a slight man with receding gray-blonde hair and pleasant features. In that instant she knew she was going to be everything he had imagined. Through the magic of their letters, they had revealed everything about themselves, and when he looked up and saw her, he flashed a smile of recognition.

The Largeness of Flowers

"...So I said to myself—I'll paint what I see—what the flower is to
me, but I'll paint it big and they will be surprised into taking the time to look
at it."

—Georgia O'Keeffe

Rising into a day shivering in a rare western gray,
clouds run ragged by wind and rain across the range,
even hottentot sun cups curled inward upon themselves,
and I became afraid the world might turn to black and white,
so I made my way to you, Georgia, inside a gallery garden
filled with the largeness of flowers, a poetry of things.

Like you I love to linger inside the bud and fold of color
upon those petal palettes, whole continents of blooms swelling
in a garden party of the grand. I think as I look in, how can you say
there is no sex in the fiery poppy, no birth in its blood rich petals,
no thought of death inside the deep and dark center, no drama
in these big beauties that dizzy and dazzle as any first love might.

You say these flowers mean nothing more than their own largeness,
lines spiraling in upon themselves and taking their natural course.
What started beneath the soil line appeared above the ground,
then plucked by you, you bequeathed it to these gallery walls.
On my wall, your wild iris blazes and poppies swell like bodies,
like any love at first sight might in some new found intimacy.

You say none of this means anything, that they are simply flowers
and big. But in the largeness of flowers I can almost see the blood rich
petals of my own mother's lips as my head tunneled past
the spread wren bone, she a sky adrift in twilight clouds, like a city
a blur in fog, the sun setting down, unaware of her own pain or of me.
My mother is dead. You are dead. The flowers return. All really big.

A garden party of the large, colossal, mammoth, but only flowers
pushing their stubborn heads toward the incessant chatter of birds.

– Andrena Zawinski

Virgin in the Manuscript

The yellow-tailed hawk
is a sign of the Virgin
addressing the lower right corner
of the manuscript.
A tiny illumination, really,
delicate in brownish ink;
the tail curves upward fetchingly.
This hawk looks as if it would harm none,
at best, an insect catcher, vermin-sweeper,
but that tiny curved beak
tells otherwise.
She's a predator
waiting to swallow
the text that consigns her
to a tight spot in the border.

– Pam Clements

Deborah Miller Rothschild

Taking a Lap With Dad

"Dad died this morning."

My brother Chris sounded as if he were in the next room although he was calling from a kitchen phone in my parents' northern California home. "I got here as quickly as I could... Peter will be down in a few hours... We can meet your plane... Mom isn't saying anything, just looking out the bedroom window."

Already the background noise echoed the business of death. A neighbor announcing the arrival of the first casserole; the visiting nurse asking questions germane to government paperwork; someone wanting to know where to put the oxygen canisters for the medical supply pick-up.

In a daze, I made reservations, packed a suitcase, and drove to the airport. My four hour plane ride from Houston to San Jose served as the final bridge between childhood and maturity.

Although it came as a shock, my father's demise didn't come as a surprise. Dad had been preparing for the end on-and-off ever since his first open-heart surgery twelve years earlier. Old photographs had been labeled, the family silver had been doled out, and he had written a book about his life. Finally, when he had done everything he needed to do and was too tired to take on anything new, Dad sat down at the worn teak kitchen table and wrote a poem about dying to his grandchildren. He put it in an envelope addressed to the youngest, walked to the mailbox, dropped it in the slot, went home, and got into bed. There he stayed for eighteen months until the morning of my brother's phone call.

Apparently my father thought he was fully prepared for his "crossing over." He had even left a manila envelope taped to the back of his closet door. It was labeled "What To Do In The Event of My Death" and contained a list that covered everything from which granddaughter should receive his mother's amethyst communion cross to what to do with his Masonic apron.

But Dad, being Dad, managed to leave out a crucial detail. Possibly it was his schoolteacher-past requiring his children to think for themselves. Perhaps it was his sense of humor. Or maybe it just didn't matter to him. But he never mentioned where he wanted his ashes to be buried.

Discussions began immediately. We quickly rejected Marshal, Michigan where he was born 83 years before, and Saratoga, California where he resided subsequent to retiring. After all, our father, a man who had lived an uncommonly rich and varied life, deserved a sendoff with more flair.

The ideas rolled out.

Would Dad like to spend eternity at Williams College? He never tired of telling stories of his undergraduate days in Williamstown. And as children we had eaten every Thanksgiving dinner off Williams College plates, always betting which one of us the college's austere first president would glower at from beneath cranberry sauce and gravy. *No, it had taken Dad an extra year to graduate so he probably wouldn't want to go back.*

Perhaps Dad would like to rest easy in Italy where, at 13, he first challenged authority and experienced a rite of passage. Accompanied by our suffragette grandmother, Dad took tea with Mussolini in an Italian garden only to be arrested by Black Shirts the following morning as he led a parade dressed in an Uncle Sam suit down the main street of Milan. *No, ever since that time he had had a recurring nightmare about Mussolini and we certainly didn't want to stir up that old ghost.*

One brother suggested a resort on the shores of the Black Sea where reputedly Dad lost his virginity to a minor Russian princess. *No, inappropriate.*

The other countered with the Hudson River Valley where our father fell in love with a co-ed from Smith College and proposed. *No, she stood him up at the altar.*

Then there was Morrow Bay where Dad had gone when he "ran away from home" in his mid-seventies in a final, futile attempt to recapture his youth. *No, it had gone badly. Dad was taken into custody by the county sheriff after he was discovered naked, huddling under a towel, on the beach. A band of wayward young men had robbed him of his worldly possessions and left him in that undignified state, shivering and claiming amnesia.*

And so it went for hours, three adult children celebrating the myths and memories of their father; stories awash with tears and brimming with laughter.

Then, almost as if prompted by Dad, the right answer hit us. "The Los Angeles Coliseum!" we shouted simultaneously.

In his youth Dad had been a runner. The 100 meter was his specialty. He had competed successfully in many regional and national track meets. Proof of his winnings still jangled on three charm bracelets in my mother's jewelry box. The heaviest by far was the bracelet hung with gold medals. Nonetheless, it was a loss in Los Angeles that marked the highlight of his track career.

In the spring of 1932, Dad competed in the United States trials for the Olympic Games. The competition was held in the Los Angeles Coliseum, newly constructed for the 10th Olympiad, which was scheduled for later that summer. But on the day of the big race Dad, not up to his usual form, placed third behind two men he had previously beaten.

Even though he had lost, my father considered himself a winner. Running in that great space gave him a triumph that lasted a lifetime. Losing to Eddie Tolan, the small black man with blistering speed, the man who later set a long standing world's record, a man who called him his friend, was in itself a badge of honor to Dad. Rather than diminish Eddie's victory, Dad never told his rival of the tendon injury he suffered just weeks before. He took the Olympic motto to heart: *The important thing in the Olympic Games is not winning but taking part. The essential thing is not conquering but fighting well.*

So it was with great excitement that the three of us planned our father's last lap. Chris, Peter, and I would put Dad in a carry-on and take an early commuter flight to Los Angeles. We would rent a car and arrive at the Los Angeles Coliseum in time to chat up the grounds crew. Surely they would warm to the idea of letting the three of us jog around the famous track as a tribute to our recently departed father. And, as we made the quarter mile run, we could casually sprinkle Dad on the infield, leaving him forever in the place where he saw his finest hour.

The plan was perfect. We loved it. Dad would have loved it.

Then, like the voice from the whirlwind, our mother decreed from her bed in the other end of the house, "Calvin will be buried next to me in my family's plot."

And so it was that my father missed his last adventure. He rests next to his wife of 53 years in the Oakland hills under the headstone, boldly etched in Times New Roman font,

CALVIN WHEELER MILLER
1910 - 1993

Memory

hangs above my computer
juxtaposing chips
and megabytes with a man
in a turban. His Afghan robe
contours crossed legs, knees
knobbing at right
angles as he sits
on a rug in his desert
encampment. We share
no name yet eyes down-
cast he radiates
the posture of my son
absorbed in a book.
My father's cheekbones
and nose haunt
the strong face.
Left hand on left knee,
his long fingers
splay as if on the frets
of my husband's guitar.
Tea steams from the cup
in his right hand.
Before him a woman
moves in his reverie.
Tendrils of smoke
part to reveal her face.
Her lips forgive,
carrying my daughter's smile
to her cheeks. Her eyes
tend the fire she
stirs with a stick.
Below them, the black
void of a photogram
where exposed whites
and grays rise
to the surface—a ring

of firing pins for a pistol
brought back from Kabul,
the tines of a fork,
sand glittering like eyes.
Ribbons of peeled cucumber
curve into Islamic
calligraphy. The glyphs
soar and twist.

– Pearl Karrer

Note: *Memory*, mixed media with
photograms on handmade paper,
30"x24"

Michael Onofrey

Fingers of Coincidence

A car rocking back and forth. The rhythm of steel wheels on steel rails. Humidity wafting through open windows. A locomotive's echo licking at the sides of the cars as they slither through a tunnel of tropical foliage.

He sits on hard wood, its surface against his buttocks and the ribs of his spine. He sits gazing down the length of the carriage, tobacco nubs and greasy food wrappers in litter, dank air swept from side to side by small overhead fans, skinny men leaning into the aisle to spit.

The door in back of him is thrown open. A woman enters and then stumbles through the car with her hands on the backs of seats, a utility of balance as if she were a bloated insect. Her purple sari exits the other end.

Jimmy gets up and grabs the swinging door in back of him. He pulls the door and it latches closed. He sits down and watches the door at the other end of the car swing back and forth. He yawns. He stretches his suntanned legs and crosses them at the ankles.

Unlike the other cubicles where six or seven or eight people sit facing each other knee to knee, Jimmy's cubicle has only one other person, a slim man who stares out the window while smoking a beedie. Jimmy had been given this reserved seat after handing the conductor ten rupees, a quick, wordless transaction while boarding the train. But the absence of bodies in his cubicle isn't the only reason for space. There is a small door, an emergency exit between the two benches that dictates more space. The slim, dark-skinned man next to the windows has his legs in front of the door, its lower half a panel of worn glaze, its upper portion a small window in a wooden frame. The window is shoved up like all the windows in the car.

The train stops. Voices outside. Someone selling bottled pop. A few dim lights with clouds of insects. Bats slicing the air. A spigot with people filling plastic bottles. A whistle. Feet moving. A man in a uniform waving a lantern. The train begins to creep. A few people standing. The cars of the train rolling. And then, the gait of the machinery returns—a familiar lullaby.

Jimmy pulls an opened pack of beedies from his shirt

pocket. A rolled leaf of tobacco is stuck between his thick lips. He strikes a wooden match. The harsh tobacco does a lot to mask the odor of the marijuana that he put into the leaf while waiting for the train. He has a ritual of rolling up ten of these special beedies before an overnight journey.

He smokes. The man at the window smokes. The train lumbers on. The lady in the purple sari comes back through the car. Jimmy gets up and closes the door after her. There is only time. There is only moist air. Another beedie. His eyelids weaken. His head rolls forward in a nod, and that's all until the wheels of the train begin to cry.

He opens his eyes and turns his head and sees nothing out the windows but black. The train slows rapidly. It stops at a raised slab of concrete. A struggling light bulb over a platform. Soft voices. The door of his cubicle swings open.

The man at the window-seat sits up and pulls his legs in. There are faces outside and one of them is the conductor who is holding a lantern and is talking to a group of people. A steel stepping stool is placed before the small door. A young woman, a girl perhaps, the line between the two wavering, appears midst the crowd of faces. She's wearing a pastel green sari and a pair of small, elegant sunglasses, as if the tint of the glasses was nothing more than a variation of reading glasses. The skin of her face, hands, and sandaled feet is smooth and white and luminous against the dark night and the dark faces that surround her.

She is somehow being thrust forward. She's up on the steel step and then up onto the floor of Jimmy's cubicle. Hands are pushing her forward and dark bodies are following her through the opening. The people in back are talking to her but she isn't answering. The man next to the window is gawking at her, his body ridged in a pair of thin trousers and a white shirt, collar soiled. She continues forward and people are entering and filling the space in back of her. Words flow softly and quickly, but are not hurried. The girl/woman sits down next to Jimmy, but it is both her will and the hands that are on her arms that determine that particular seat.

Jimmy is on the girl's right. A man with stretched, weathered skin is on her left. The slim man at the window is opposite this man. Next to the slim man there is a middle-aged woman in a flower-print dress, her body with comfortable weight. Next to her and directly opposite Jimmy is a skinny man, creased skin, complexion from an outdoor occupation.

Outside, the conductor closes the little door, sticks his hand through the window and flips a latch on the inside. The conductor's face disappears after he steps down from the stepping stool. There is a whistle. A door slams. The train creaks forward and as it gains speed the conductor appears and stands and exchanges a few words with the man across from Jimmy, language efficient, yet gentle. This brief conversation ends with a nod and a polite smile.

The newcomers talk among themselves in a volume of whispers. Jimmy looks away, looks across the aisle to where all the men have their heads turned and are looking at the girl. The next group in their cubicle have their heads twisted and are looking. A man in the compartment in front stands and looks over the seatback. He sits down quickly. Someone walks by and looks, then turns and walks back to where he came from. The newcomers continue to talk while ignoring the attention. Then, little by little, people stop looking.

The conversation among the four narrows to two, and then tapers to nothing. Jimmy's eyes look down at his lap to where his vision can see the girl's hands folded on her lap. Her wrists and hands are slim but they don't lack nutrition. Her skin is hairless and smooth and seems to glow, for its tone hasn't been scarred by the sun, nor by any labor of household like those displayed by the woman sitting opposite the girl. Jimmy's eyes go back to the aisle of the car, people having turned away, turned back into themselves and the late hour, turned back into the sound and rhythm of the train.

Jimmy forgoes his stiff posture and slides an inch or two down to allow his long body a slight angle on the hard seat. The young woman next to him tenses. She has a slight angle to her head as if she were waiting for something, but Jimmy only looks at the man in front of him, the man's dark eyes relaxed and wilting, whites smudged red.

There are moments of nothing. Just sitting. Then, the girl's right hand moves smoothly to her right over the fabric that covers her leg. Her hand falls to the small bit of seat that separates her from Jimmy. It sits there as if stalled, as if waiting, but there is nothing except for the cadence of the train. Slowly, the hand drifts, and her slim, white fingers come to the outside of Jimmy's thigh, the worn hem of his khaki shorts just above where she makes contact.

Jimmy's eyes have already looked down. He has watched her hand as it moved from the middle of her lap. He hasn't moved his body. Only his gray eyes.

Her fingertips jump, jump at the hair on the skin of his thigh. Her fingers curl into a fist as if she's touched something hot. Her hand stays clinched and poised. Then nothing. And more nothing. And then her slim fingers unwrap and reach out. She feels the hair on his suntanned leg. Her fingers stop. Then move through the hair and over the skin in a small area no larger than her fingers' reach. Her fingertips move quickly and delicately while concentrating on what's at each soft pad. They hurry, hurry not to get caught, hurry for information, hurry with curiosity, but they are unable to shortcut perception which is flickering like electricity. Her fingertips move not to tell him something but to tell her something.

Her head is bent as if she were listening to a secret. Then, her fingers stop, and then her hand returns to her lap. She waits, waits for someone to notice, waits for someone to say something, waits for embarrassment. She waits for the sounds which don't come from the others. They are asleep. She waits longer. And then her hand moves back to Jimmy's bare leg.

She begins with the same small area, then branches out. Her fingertips go lightly and nimbly like small fibers of current. They go down to his knee and search that area, the line between hair and no-hair explored. She extends her arm and her fingers find more hair below the knee. Her hand goes back to his knee, then proceeds upward to on top of his thigh. Her manicured fingers spread and her palm comes down to hover on his soft, spongy hair. Her fingers curve slightly and then her hand moves around inside and then outside to measure the girth of his muscle.

Jimmy's eyes are wide. He watches her hand at his thigh. Then her delicate fingers are on the coarse fabric of his shorts. She's not so interested in the cloth, but she roams. She finds his left forearm. Again, there is a sudden stopping. She's found more hair, more soft, bleached hair on his arm. Her fingers move, then dance all over the stringy muscle of his forearm until they are tapping at his wrist.

Jimmy turns his head slowly, his skull rotating on his neck. He looks at her face. There are no lines but her lips are almost smiling.

Her fingers venture onto the back of his left hand. She is meticulous, careful, and attentive.

Jimmy looks at the rise of her chest. She is at least in puberty, but probably at the end of it, or maybe over it, for her age is a changing perception. His eyes twist and turn and shove their gaze through her light brown hair which is under a transparent fold of her sari. Then his eyes feel through her brown eyebrows just over her gold, wire-rim sunglasses. Her nose, mouth, cheeks and ears are without blemish. Smooth, protected skin, almost pink, a translucent brown from beneath.

Her fingers are now scampering over and through his fingers. The sensitive pads of her fingertips are exploring the ends of his fingernails. They stop. Then they retrace a path up his arm.

He turns the angle of his head so he's not looking so much at her, yet she remains in his periphery. He's assumed a less conspicuous pose.

At his upper arm her fingers, and then her hand, go around his muscle, and then over and around the ball of his shoulder which is under a cotton shirt. Her hand moves across the fabric and finds his exposed collarbone. She follows this raised line and stops where she again finds hair. Her fluttering fingers send chills all over Jimmy's flesh. For a moment, her fingers tangle themselves in his chest hair. Then they go down further and find more of a thicket where his shirt comes together in a V. She tilts her head even more as if there were a question, a deeper, more puzzling question about what she has found sitting next to her on a train in the middle of the night in the middle of Sri Lanka.

Her white, slim fingers come up and flit around his neck until they are at a map of stubble under his jaw. She goes over this in a quick recognizance. Her hand is now on his face, her fingertips looking feverishly for form and texture. They linger and they dance over his lips, but then they brush his thick mustache. She stops. Then she continues. She spends time measuring length and width and curl. She moves on to his cheeks and nose.

Jimmy sits as if posing for a painting. He closes his eyes. Her light finger-touches continue up. She goes over his eyelids. She goes over his eyebrows and forehead and into his bleached hair. She finds his ear. Her hand drifts down along his neck and on down until she is back at his leg, his thick, hairy thigh. She pauses, and then removes her hand and places it back on her lap. Her head straightens. She sits.

There is time. She is sitting and he is sitting. Everyone else is sleeping, heads thrown this way and that as if their necks were broken. Jimmy is looking straight ahead—a hundred thousand lingering touches.

A conductor with a ticket punch enters the car at the far end. His assistant wears a lesser uniform. They wake people one cubicle at a time. Noise and movement slowly comes down the car.

The conductor says something to Jimmy's cubicle. Jimmy says, "My ticket?" The girl jumps at the sound of Jimmy's voice. She jumps as if having encountered something absolutely alien. Jimmy glances and sees fear folding her face. She brings her body in towards itself in defense. The middle-aged lady reaches across and puts a hand on the girl's knee. She says something to the girl. The girl remains tense. Jimmy gives the conductor a ticket. The man across from Jimmy is getting tickets from his pocket. Jimmy is given back his ticket.

The conductor moves on, moves out of the car. People settle. Broken snoring resumes. Heads fall limp. Slowly, tentatively, after half an hour, the girl's slim arm with its whisper of pastel green fabric relaxes against Jimmy's arm.

At five in the morning at a stop in the jungle with birds venturing noises and the train panting next to a slab of cement, the girl and her three companions get off the train. The small door is latched. There is a whistle. The train pulls away. Jimmy leans and looks. Quickly, nothing remains, silence except for the train, black except for a few feet of reflection, a few flits of smoke from the engine.

Jimmy sits for twenty minutes. Then he gets up and walks to the dining car. He buys a glass of spicy tea from a skinny young man who's wearing a thin, dirty T-shirt. Jimmy walks over and sits down on a hard, small seat at a small table, the surface of the table damp and greasy.

He sits alone, an empty car with only a skinny young man staring at him from behind a counter of worn Formica. Jimmy sips tea and looks out an opened window, warm air brushing his face.

Darkness turning gray, then glowing red. Jimmy watches, a slight smile on his face, eyes stretched, a half-filled glass of tepid tea in his hand. He has the pulsing of rails. He has the movement of birds. He has what he hasn't seen before.

The Line

Now that we have secured this line,
we'll pull it tight across the belly of the earth
bulging on either voluptuous side.

Look how it leads out of sight
past the beaming horizon
and the irresolute night

faltering like a tattered flag.
It's a clothes-line you can hang
anything on, to dangle in the breeze,

to dance the fandango,
swift as you please,
to tangle in the branches

of the lowering trees,
to scorch or freeze,
depending upon the season.

We sit and stare at it for hours.
It does not end.
It is our friend.

It slithers like a rattler
across the terrain.
No matter.

I'm going out to hang my soaking tears
right there. Soon they'll dry
one by one in the arid air.

It's your turn now.
Grab a handful from your basket
of hopes and clothespins,

lost laundry and soggy souls.
Bye and bye everything
can be taken down and folded away.

Except for the line.
Outlasting our leaving,
it goes on just fine.

– Ansie Baird

Stitches in Time Serve Memory and Vision

IN COMMEMORATION OF THE ONE HUNDRED YEARS PLUS
ONE ANNIVERSARY OF THE ROSWELL PARK CANCER
INSTITUTE 1903-2004

1

I am The Women's Journey For A Cure Quilt:
I honor women in every department from
"parking lot to pathology."[1]
Everyone who looks into me may see herself—
no position is ordinary—from Nobel Laureate
to Human Resources.

2

The quilters work in silence. "Their rhythms
are a musical science."[2]
Immersed in technique, their voices break open their lives...
They aim for perfection, but I reflect their humanity.
"There's always the humility block, the one that gets
put on the wrong way."[3]

3

I *am* their masterpiece—the cottage sampler.
I take shape in blocks:
see my seven eightpointed stars, one gray and rose,
another royal blue around a square.
see double red chimneys on the two-storied house.
Another of my twenty blocks is a stained glass
window design with yellow flower.
At my top, centered, a vertical, rectangular
block is four poplar leaves whose stems
connect to a small circle.
A block of two black microscopes, diagonal
to each other, are joined to yellow cells with blue
nucleuses on a scarlet background.

To my far, upper right is an evergreen
tree of hope on a pinafore of white.
I spread out shaped by the quilters'
skilled hands, the blendings of colors and shapes
in relationship, a symphony of choices...

4

I am your heartfelt brain, the untold story—
the myriad decisions and stitches—the Quest...
I am the Past and the Present made visible.
I am *your* quilt celebrating your discoveries
and your Hope.
I am your Dream made touchable.
I wrap myself around each patient with care.
I am your Soul's proud window.

– Jimmie Margaret Gilliam

---

[1]Carolyn Coles Benton
[2]Marija Vujcic
[3]Bernadette Keitz

Pulling Poe Out Of Baltimore

Beneath black jackets and books
we turn our backs on the city
with its back-alley gossip
and its rabid dogs.
It is another humid day
wearing an overcast blanket.
There's a raven tattooed on my heart
though most think it's a crow.
We make an odd couple
waiting here for a train—
his frail frame and pallor
to my darkness. He is sober
and thinking of penning the great opus
he's buried in his mind for years.
I never like being stepped on.
The tall tombstones of this town
are no place for us. We know
that these people will gossip us
down to a drunk and a stain.

– J.P. Dancing Bear

Lynn Veach Sadler

The Two Alices

I loved The Girl instantly. What was not to love? Body Beautiful and then some. Rima the Bird Girl. Simple, shy. First impressions.

A Company fete. In D.C., oddly enough, and not Langley. I was between postings. I should have been kowtowing and assertively-aggressively making my next way. But I was tired of it all. I took my drink and wandered out into the garden. Gardens.

She was by herself. A ventriloquist from the sound of it. Sounds.

"You're talking to the flowers." Mr. Smooth was I. "You'd better watch yourself in the nosegays. I walked out in my small garden one day and was bitten by a petunia." Mr. Smoother was I.

She didn't turn to look at me. "Actually, the flowers were talking to *me*."

Who was having on *whom* here? "So, what are they saying, these flowers?"

"That they talk all the time when they meet a person worth talking to and that all flowers would talk if we didn't make their beds too soft and keep them sleeping. They consider it bad manners for them to talk first."

That jostled something way deep in the still-unpickled *expanse* of my brain. "I've heard that before. Let's see...it's...*Alice in Wonderland* maybe?"

"You refer, I believe, to *Alice's Adventures in Wonderland* and had best have said our exchange thus far has trickled through your head like water through a sieve. Still, you were close. The flowers that talk are from *Through the Looking Glass*."

"Ah, hare of the Dodgson that bit me as a child."

"Alice, rather, I think. She chased the—*rabbit*, if you don't mind my saying so."

"White. With pink ears. And I believe that I am chasing you. That I'd give you an un-birthday present 365 days of the year, even on your birthday. That said flowers are correct in assessing you as a person worth talking to. Do they *jabber wockyly*, by the way?"

"No, the flowers have no freedom to bear arms (or legs), only freedom of speech. As for me, I have no 'Eat Me' signs marked out in currants. No 'Drink Me' signs about my person. I'll not shrink or grow to suit *you*. Still, I do not rule out eyes. It's only that few modern men are masters of their eyes. Or *any* of their senses."

"And I thought you thought we men were merely senses with no intelligence, central or otherwise. But is it *words* I should master, perhaps? Who was it who said the mastering bit? The Cheshire Cat? Did the Cheshire Cat grin and *bare* it?"

"By the italics I *heard*, I've mastered your spelling. *B-a-r-e*."

"You have it, nuts and *bare* bolts. But I still want—"

"'The question is,' said Alice, 'whether you CAN make words mean so many different things.' *And*—'The question is,' said Humpty Dumpty, 'which is to be master—that's all.'"

I was smug. "Thanks. I'll never be able to put that together again."

"Never mind. As the Duchess told Alice, 'Take care of the sense, and the sounds will take care of themselves.' Did you know Charles Lutwidge Dodgson was born in Cheshire?"

"Is that why—?"

She merely shrugged.

"Sorry, but I have to go."

"Back inside to the party, you mean? 'Will you, won't you, will you, won't you, will you join the dance? Will you, won't you, will you, won't you, won't you join the dance?'"

"I am presently ill-equipped to join *your* dance, though my heart waltzes that way. No, I'm going home. I want to read the two Alices before I see you again *at lunch tomorrow*."

"You can download the two Alices easily enough. But shouldn't it be tea?"

"By the time you arrive, I'll be as mad as the Hatter having tea."

"The moral of which is, 'The more there is of mine, the less there is of yours.'"

"I predict that's not the way it's going to be for us. Neither of us is going to get lost in the translation of the other."

"Translation? Go slowly if not 'gentle' into this good night."

"Pardon, but aren't you mixing poets?"

"Doubtless.   I was also saying goodnight.   But, doubtless, Dylan Thomas was an ardent fan of Lewis Carroll, too."

"Doubtless."

"As the Duchess said, 'I quite agree with you, and the moral of that is—"Be what you would seem to be"—or if you'd like it put more simply—"Never imagine yourself not to be otherwise than what it might appear to others that what you were or might have been was not otherwise than what you had been would have appeared to them to be otherwise."'"

"The translation of which I am indeed lost in.   Until tomorrow, then."

. . .

We were married three months later and would have resigned from the Company, had it not allowed us to work as a team.   Permission was not easily secured, though we argued, and it was quite true, that "safe houses" often benefited from appearing to be occupied by "regular married couples" and that "for-your-eyes-only" communications worked especially well for couples.   She was in Intelligence (analysis) but wanted to join me in DO (The Directorate of Operations).   Already savvy in trade-craft, together, we would add up to more than two no matter what we were tasked with.

I have to tell you, she had gleaned stuff (e.g., Arab mud men, SAVAK—the Iranian Secret Police) from the gossip of insider wives and such that made me fear for our own Alice's imaginative reach.   She *brilliged mimsyly* of such faux pas as serving Buddhists meat; of revenge by increasing the level of pele-pele and other hot peppers in curries and assorted foods; of Cambodians drowning birds in cages, throwing them in woks to cook and singe off the feathers, and holding them by their beaks while eating the rest of their bodies.   She knew about "red rice" and the "van man."   I was thinking how mild the two Alice books were in comparison when she launched into an episode from, as she put it, "her thirteenth year"   Her parents had taken her for a picnic in the Khyber Pass between Pakistan and Afghanistan.   In a desolate stretch inhabited, to all intents and purposes, by giant boulders, they had suddenly been surrounded by some forty Afghans, who sat in a circle watching the family as it ate. Had she not charmed them by taking off her hat and filling it with food to pass among them, the family would probably have been killed. As it was, her elders carried back intelligence explaining why both the British and the Russians have been thwarted in their efforts to conquer Afghanistan and useful in the present hostilities, while the grins on the faces of these Afghans recalled to their daughter the Cheshire Cat. The rest, as they say, is history; the rest, as *we* say, is *Alice*. I have never seen Company interlocutors so completely flummoxed; I have never felt so flummoxed myself.

She also brought impressive credentials to the bargaining table. Both of her parents had served under different administrations as members of the PFIAB (President's Foreign Intelligence Advisory Board). She claimed to be distantly related to Virginia Hall, the one-legged World War II intelligence agent who became one of the Company's first female operations officers. If that hadn't been enough, she confided to me that she was going to claim to know the true identity of "355," the female member of the famous Culper Ring during the American Revolution.

We wore our superiors down, finally, with our insistence that we truly were much of a muchness and that our "Alicing," as we had chosen to call it, was potentially as good as Navajo Code Talking. To wit:

Why is a raven like a writing desk?

"I see what I eat." vs. "I eat what I see."

"I like what I get." vs. "I get what I like."

"I breathe when I sleep." vs. "I sleep when I breathe."

The Fish-Footman's "For the Duchess. An invitation from the Queen to play croquet." vs. The Frog-Footman's "From the Queen. An invitation for the Duchess to play croquet."

The deciding factor was our pointing out that the world really is laid out like a large chessboard or, contrariwise and curiouser and curiouser, a croquet field, where the balls can be construed as live hedgehogs, the mallets as live flamingoes, and soldiers are always doubling themselves up and standing upon their hands and feet to make arches.

I was officially "Tweedledum"; my wife, "Tweedledee." We came to be known, informally, as "The Two Alices." As operatives, we were awesome. As husband and wife, we were beyond awesome.

Then came 9/11. Her cover was assistant to Saira Shah, who made the documentary *Beneath the Veil* with the help of RAWA, a school for Afghan girls in the Khaiwa refugee camp in northwestern Pakistan. I was "doing my thing" not just in Afghanistan but Turkmenistan, Uzbekistan, and Tajikistan, among others, and was in and out of such cities as Kandahar, Jalalabad, Zaranj, and Mazar-e-Sharif. We still don't know what went wrong. Her messages and letters abruptly stopped. The Company wouldn't let me go to where she'd last been.

Saira Shah, some months later, found this last communication hidden in a scroll, in Arabic, that had been presented to her when she left RAWA.

Dearest T. D.,

I can't explain myself because I'm not myself. A hill is a valley, which is nonsense if you like, but I've now heard nonsense, compared with which, that would be as sensible as a dictionary.

As our mutual friend unwittingly said to the mouse of the long, sad tale, the question is, "Ou est ma chatte?" (What's the French for "fiddle-de-dee"? I am still able to speak in French when I can't think of the English for a thing, to turn out my toes as I walk, and to remember who I am and, more important, who you are.) *Ma chatte* is lurking, grin and all. As the Walrus said, the time has [almost] come. I feel like one of the oysters who joined the Walrus and the Carpenter, but, contrariwise, I know that I won't make myself a bit realer by crying. I should, though, appreciate a rubdown in Roland's Macassar Oil, which is in long senescence here, though you have absented yourself from it. You will remember that I, like our mutual friend, always had trouble managing my flamingo.

At this juncture, I find that the real question is not the difference between the White Rabbit and the March Hare, but between the Hatter and the latter, both, you may assume, being mad of mind and temperament. The axis readies axes. That, at least, should not pose a knot, for a dreadfully ugly child makes a rather handsome pig still.

This, you may surmise, is a place of some enchantment, abounding in magic mushrooms and gardens in which the gardeners must always be painting the white roses red. The smoke alone is worth a thousand pounds a puff (and this language, should you care to translate it, is worth a thousand pounds a word). I know you wish to know how I like the Queen, and I am dying to tell you. The answer is, not at all, for she's so extremely—likely to win. She doesn't know what you mean by *your* way, for *all* ways about here belong to her. I had hoped she would appeal on my behalf, if only for our sexual consanguinity, but it has taken all the running I could do to keep in the same place, no matter that I curtsied and curtsied while thinking what to say.

I expect that my shoes will no longer be done with blacking. Only the Gryphon knows where boots and shoes are done with whiting and made of soles and eels, as any shrimp could tell you.

Please remember, T.D., not only that flamingoes and mustard both bite but that the moral of this homily is "Birds of a feather flock together," which is nothing to what I could say if I chose. I can confirm that the Duchess was correct in inferring two morals: love makes [has made] the [our] world go round; and, if you take care of the sense, [my] sounds will do their utmost to take care of themselves.

I will try to remember the lessons of our turtle, who was called Tortoise because he taught us. I will try hardest to remember the lessons of Drawling-Master, hoping against hope that the reason they are called "lessons" is not that they "lessen" from day to day. You do remember that old conger-eel who taught Drawling, Stretching, and Fainting in Coils? I hope I prove no dodo. Already, I seem to understand why our good Classics Master taught both Laughing and Grief. I would not beg pardon, knowing as we do that it isn't respectable to beg. If I do succumb to begging, I will beg a biscuit to quench my thirst. Yet I am glad that this is one dance you will not be asked to join. Oh, if they bake me too brown, I will have to sugar my hair! I will keep my ear on the prize: when I get to the Eighth Square, I shall be a queen. In a sense, we began, à la Hatter, with the twinkling of tea accompanied by The Two T's. We always knew that we must begin at the beginning and go on till we came to the end, then stop. Still, I remain the Eaglet for English, the Gryphon for "Hjckrrh," and the Anglo-Saxon Messenger for "Haigha." You and I were often at dinn—oh, guess where Dinn may be! But if you translate my love too late, know that I keep the loving heart of childhood (and beyond!). It will not be lost in your translation.

I know that you know, T. D., most of our friend's poems to have a relation with fish, for no wise fish goes anywhere without a porpoise, and in this company was once a "fish squeezing unit." I close with a poor poem, but mine own, looking to your future. Though it is lacking in fish, try to find some contentment in its scales.

Here and now is the rule for tomorrow:
Jam yesterday and jam tomorrow—
but never jam today.

You don't deserve tomorrow
if you haven't believed
as many as six impossible things
before breakfast today;
if you've never floated down a rabbit hole
or through the Mist of Dissolving
into the Looking-Glass World;
if flowers and a bread-and-butterfly
haven't talked with you today;
if you haven't, today,
committed three tomorrowly puns,
ceased to think in chorus,
and borogoved outgrabely.

Tomorrow says,
"It's a poor sort of memory
that only works backwards."

Yours,

T. D., too/two

P.S.
Look for me among the flowers where the beds are hard.

I was debriefed, of course, for we were down to one Alice, and only an Alice could know of a certainty what the other Alice meant. I translated what the Company needed to know (knew to need). But I made sure that that which was "for my heart only" was lost in the translation.

Vissi d'arte

This one was safe, he had a madonna
on the dash, warning *va adagio papa—*
Daddy go slow. He slowed and I jumped in.
Umbria passed in the sultry afternoon
as we sang along with Tosca.
A music lover, but he was not safe,
no more than the Manchester pigeon fanciers,
or the ruddy young priest in Connemara.
Get in the back, puttana madonna.

We stopped at a distant house he knew,
whitewashed stone, where on a terrace
facing the highway his wife gave me
a glass of water to drink with a cool slice of lime.
In the days when I lived for love and art,
the lime and her look redeemed my heart.

– Ruth Holzer

Dorothy Stone

Whose Refugees

PICTURE POSTCARD DURING THE BALKAN WARS, c.1993
Quartz sandstone figurine, c. 7000 BC, Belgrade Nat'l Museum, Serbia

Ego swollen head,
even then cataract'd eyes
that avoid admission,
lowered orbs unseeing
while haunted children's eyes
all through the Balkans
blink
and capture a horror for a lifetime.

70th century BC.
BC! My God! Blind then, too!

Until a few years ago, it had never occurred to me, with my comfortable American assumptions, that members of any extended family of mine would be victims of a civil war—or would become, as a result, political casualties. But in February of 1992, I met my first refugees, my son-in-law's parents.

They had made the difficult choice of leaving their home in Bihac, Bosnia, to come to America, after the shelling of their town became unbearable, even in their own particular haven, a garage partially underground where they retreated when things got heavy. It had been solidly built for their tractor some years before, and neighbors had laughingly called it the bunker, until they, these years later, sought refuge there too. But then came the day when, with two plastic bags of belongings, the elderly couple left their land and, after a brief stop in a refugee camp, flew to America where they moved into their son's and my daughter's small house in New York, thankful to be able to sleep through the night without fear.

A year later a cousin and her three children arrived and temporarily moved in as well. The cousin's husband had been killed the second day of the war while attempting to deliver food to the fighters. She had eventually found someone to fly her and her children out of the country in a small plane and, from a temporary refugee camp, made the arrangements for New York.

Then there was the high school exchange student whose parents told her it was better not to come home, and who therefore needed summer lodgings until the new school year.

And finally, once the fatherless family had found a place of their own and started on their new lives, another cousin arrived from Sarajevo. She, like her relatives before her, had locked the door to her home and had left with one small bag of belongings, not wanting people to know she was leaving forever. Once here, she loved being able to switch on a light when it started to get dark. In Sarajevo candles had become luxury items, incredibly expensive, to be hoarded and used carefully. But as the siege went on, she could no longer bear to sit night after night in the dark, so she sat with a candle, literally watching her money disappear, but she refused to snuff out the light.

My daughter's house has been empty of refugees for some time now. Only one of the temporaries chose to return to the damaged home she left. One died and had to be buried here in this land where people spoke a strange language. The rest, at home now in America, are busy rewriting their personal histories.

That war is done. Other disasters and world problems have taken over the headlines, and today the news and our memories are again filled with sights that we all would like to forget, the ghastly glow of burning, crumbling buildings here in our own country; torched villages abroad; exploding bombs; exploding people. Footage from far too many areas in the world shows bereft faces, refugees beautiful in their exhaustion, heart-rending in their mute cry for help. Refugees who may never have the choice of whether to return or not, refugees destined to live or die in places other than on their home soil. Then there are those who will never have the dubious comfort of being actual refugees—call them life's refugees if you will—who make whatever compromises necessary in order to survive, in the meantime perhaps building up resentment toward those who have a more charmed life.

THIRD WORLD BLUES

Oh, Democracy,
oh, Capitalism,
oh, yes.

Our mouth waters
at the thought of eating
at your table.
The menu tantalizes:
caviar scoops
on lemon ice,
chilled, chived vichyssoise,
honey-glazed sesame salmon
on a bed of couscous,
asparagus risotto with dried cherries,
fresh fruit plate and Gorgonzola,
chocolate decadence cake
slathered in raspberry sauce. . .
But for now,
saliva runs
in our streets.
We'll eat at anyone's table.
A bowl of thin soup will do.
Any thin creed too.

I wonder if we are going to allow history, personal, national and moral, to be rewritten the way refugees have had to recast their lives. Responsibility must be taken by someone. By us? We can't wait for all of the Serbs to take it, the warlords to take it, the terrorists. There will be no time to wait for that. I know it's hateful lumping all Serbs together, all Muslims who support suicide missions together, or any other group one doesn't understand, but it's hard not to fall into that pattern when reading, for instance, of Slobodan Milosevic at The Hague, denying responsibility for what happened in Kosovo; according to his rendering of events, he and his brand of Yugoslavians were, once again in history, the victims.

But then I stop myself from this particular profiling and remember a story told by Miep Gies, the woman who brought food to the family of Anne Frank when they were in hiding, the woman who saved Anne's diary. Looking back on that horrible time, she warned of the dangers of lumping people together and condemning whole groups, as she had found herself doing after the war when the hiding place of the Frank family became a tourist attraction, and she saw a group of Germans leaving the area after their tour. Out of control, she began screaming at

them, at how obscene they—the Nazis—were, at how they had
no right to violate this place. As she said when telling the story,
"I really gave it to them." It was only later that she was told they
were Germans who had been in concentration camps—for
standing up against what was being done in their country by
Hitler and his followers.

　　　　We can try our best not to generalize. We can try to
accept that in an imperfect world individuals can be monsters.
And yet, how can we also accept that so many in the name of
ethnic identity or religious pride or patriotic fervor continue to
follow those leaders, and do monstrous deeds in the name of
country or cause? That is the question we and history have a
right to ask. So far, why is it that the only answers that we have
heard are of justification—that bad things have been done to
Serbs in the past, that Muslims have been humiliated, that there
are prior historical claims to consider, that vengeance is
"theirs"—whoever "they" are that particular year. While we
wait for our answers, more men, women and children have been
trying to make the trek to sanctuary, to homes that opened their
doors to them if they were lucky, to camps if not.

TEMPORARY HOUSING

In transition?
Between borders?
Wars?

Collapsible easy assembly canvas homes
without heat, lights or water.
Possibility of heavy snow
for extra insulation,
can also be melted for water supply
if heat source found.
Cozy proximity encourages
intimate understanding
of family and neighbors
in otherwise inhospitable land.

Waiting list.
Limited openings.
Hurry.

Our world, hardly recovered from a decade of devastation, pain, displacement and death, then found Iraq and its aftermath front and center. Radio, TV, newspapers, magazines all filled us with images and facts and strategy. More, really, than we could absorb. More than we liked to admit into our daily lives.

Are we, in this proud 21st century of ours—as was the artifact back in 7000 BC—blind, too? Deliberately unseeing? Refugees from responsibility? Those are perhaps the painful questions we can no longer allow ourselves to ignore.

Acknowledgment: "Third World Blues" appeared in Poets' Paper, spring, 1999.

Journey to the Present—From Russia to America

I've been a child's innocence,
    not knowing how short it would live.
I've been a cancerous country,
    contaminating its European neighbors
    not knowing how ill, myself, I've been.
I've been a painted bread truck
    carrying *enemies of the people* in my belly,
    not knowing that passers-by
    were oblivious to my cargo.
I've been a sport arena with a huge stage,
    resonating the steps and voices of great poets,
    not knowing that their souls were doomed.
I've been a revolt-banner,
    hanging from a dissident's balcony
    not knowing that in five short minutes
    its letters would be torn off and scattered,
    and would become medicine for my bitter land.
I've been a loud cry for help,
    that spasms the throat of the country,
    not knowing that a gag would silence me
    for another decade before I escaped suffocation.
I've been a train from Vienna to Rome,
    whistling, laughing, rumbling
    through the free outer space
    not knowing where would be my depot.

I am a museum of Ellis Island,
    knowing thousands of footprints
    of burdens and hopes.
I am road sand on the filigreed map of the world.

– Natalia Zaretsky

Gary Earl Ross

Battle Babies

"Hello, Rebecca."

"Alan. It's been a long time."

"Yes, it has. Is this seat taken?"

"Edward couldn't come. I guess I was saving it for you."

"Thank you."

"Marcus thought you'd be here yesterday for Family Day. What happened?"

"Screwy weather. A severe tornado warning shut down the airports in Columbia and Augusta. I had to fly into Charleston late and rent a car. It was way past muster when I got here last night so I went straight to my hotel."

"I told him it must be something like that."

"I tried to get a message to him earlier, to let him know what was happening."

"He never got it. At least not before I left him. But then, after dinner, he had me take him and three of his battle buddies to the ATM on base and then to the big PX. It would've been hard to get a message to him there."

"Battle buddies?"

"Part of their training. They learn to work in groups and pairs, to depend on each other in combat."

"Oh. So what were his battle buddies like?"

"Nice kids, actually. Two white boys, one from Kansas and one from Missouri, and a boy named Hernandez from Florida. The PX was like any Wal-Mart or Big K. It was the first time in nine weeks these kids had been in a store. They went nuts—sneakers, jeans, jerseys, CDs. Marcus bought me a scarf and a purse and Edward a pen set. He got you a book, the newest hardcover in that mystery series you like so much. You don't have it yet, do you?"

"No."

"Good. Anyway, we were there till he had to report, 8:30—or 20:30, as he corrected me."

"I don't think he'd have got my message anyway. I never got past the switchboard. But they did tell me what gate to use and what time to be here this morning."

"Marcus will be so glad to see you."

"I wouldn't have missed it, Bec. How many times does your only son graduate from basic training?"

"None, if you're lucky."

"You know what I mean."

"Yes, I do. I just wish . . ."

"I know. I wish college had worked out too."

"It's not that he flunked out."

"No, he didn't."

"He just didn't like it."

"College isn't for everybody."

"And he felt so out of place in Vermont."

"He's a biracial kid from Cleveland, Rebecca. Of course he felt out of place in Vermont."

"The job offer was too good to pass up, Alan."

"I know. I know. We've had this discussion before. No need to have it again."

"Well, after Marcus came home, *his* job opportunities were limited."

"They were no better when he came to live with us. He hated the call center but he liked working at the Rock and Roll Hall of Fame. Getting laid off was a real surprise."

"He said being unemployed was too stressful, for him and for you and Karen."

"That's for sure."

"When he told me he was going to enlist, he said we always told him he could be anything he wanted, but he needed more specific suggestions. He said he hoped the Army would give him the structure and discipline he lacked."

"He said that?"

"Yes, or something like it."

"Well, the Army made my cousin Ann's son grow up. He went back to school afterward."

"If Marcus ever goes back, at least he'll have a year's worth of credits to transfer."

"And G.I. money."

"That's something to look forward to."

"Yes, it is."

"And Cassandra did so well at Spellman."

"Cassie's a different person."

"Have you talked to her lately?"

"Two days ago. I know she can't come because the baby

and Eric have both been sick."

"I'm flying out to visit her from here."

"She didn't tell me that."

"I'll be there only a few days."

"First South Carolina and then Los Angeles. I bet it'll be hard to go back to December in Vermont. By the way, what's happening to your classes while you're taking all this time off?"

"My graduate assistant is covering till I get back. What about you? How's your business?"

"Slow. Fewer housing starts mean fewer calls for electrical contractors. Nobody'll get a Christmas bonus this year but I'm getting enough business to keep the office open."

"That's good. How's Karen?"

"She's fine."

"And your little girl?"

"Claudia is a handful. She's into gymnastics and piano lessons."

"How old is she now?"

"She'll be nine next month, and she just *adores* her big brother."

"Nine. Hmm."

"What?"

"That's the same age as Marcus when . . . you know."

"Yeah."

"It *has* been a long time."

"Yes. How's Edward?"

"He's fine. Semi-retired, finally, so he spends less time in Boston."

"That's good. Is he gonna take up skiing?"

"At his age? I doubt it. Besides, he's not all that comfortable in Vermont either."

"Oh."

"We'll go someplace warmer when I retire. I'm too old to give up tenure and start over."

"Of course."

"Four or five more years and then we'll relocate. I may teach a course or two somewhere, but I'm staying out of school politics, union politics, community politics, and grantwriting."

"Sounds like a plan to me. Hey, listen to that."

"What?"

"The music."

"Oh."

"They're piping in an oldies station."

"Yes."

"'Excuse me while I touch the sky . . .'"

"Not too loud. There are people around."

"Back in college, when we were toking up and marching for civil rights and against 'Nam, did you ever think we'd be listening to Hendrix doing 'Purple Haze' at an Army base?"

"No, I can't say I did . . . Look, way out there, at the edge of the woods. They're getting into formation. It's going to start soon."

"Wish I'd brought my binoculars. They are going to pass these bleachers, aren't they?"

"Yes."

"Do you know where Marcus will be? I brought my digital camera."

"The first group, A company, but I don't think they'll be close enough for a good picture. Besides, the sun's right in front of us. When it's over, they'll be at the far end of the field. There'll be signs for each company, so we can find him there and take pictures. Don't worry, though. He'll be easy to spot during the ceremony. He's getting the company marksmanship medal."

"Wow. He sent me his first target, and I was amazed at how well he did at 300 meters. I hung it up in the office, and some of the guys started calling him Hawkeye. A medal, huh?"

"Yes. On his final qualifier he got the top score, 39 out of 40 shots."

"Really? Hawkeye is right. Did he say anything about sniper training? I think snipers get to nest in safer places . . . I mean, I think they don't put them right on the front line and—oh, God. Did he talk to you about . . . about what happens next?"

"After his Advanced Infantry Training?"

"Yes."

"He said there's a good chance he's going to Iraq."

"He told me that a month ago. He said he didn't know how he was going to tell you."

"He told me yesterday. He just told me and said not to worry. It's all I thought about in the hotel last night."

"I know what you mean. All I could think about was the irony."

"Irony?"

"Do you know what he wanted me to bring him from home?"

"What?"

"And I brought 'em too. Got three bags in my jacket pockets. He used to walk Claudia to the store and they'd come back with their mouths full and two bags apiece."

"What?"

"Gummi bears."

"You're kidding."

"No. Here he is getting a marksmanship medal and going off to some godforsaken patch of earth and he wants kid candy."

"They're all so young, Alan."

"It's a damn shame that babies fight wars. Babies always fight wars."

"Yes, but this time it's our baby."

"And this war makes no sense at all. Next November, regime change, right here."

"Until Marcus is back with one of us, that won't matter. Until he's somewhere I can hop on a plane and see him and hold him . . ."

"I know."

"Gummi bears, huh?"

"Got 'em right here. Want some?"

"You brought them for Marcus."

"I've got three bags, remember? Somehow I don't think he'll mind if we share one. Come on, hold out your hand."

While Your Back was Turned

Someone thrusts her squalling infant,
a packet of inconsolability,
into your startled arms.
You clasp him to your chest,
your legs begin their old
easy bob and weave,
your throat its croon and murmur.

You place your face
against his sorrowing head,
catch again the dizzy whiff
of infancy, hold on tight,
one hand enclosing
his small bottom, the other
stroking his grieving cheek.

And here you are,
lurching the rutted road of recollection,
seeking to hush this bundle
into slumber. What happened
while your back was turned?
How is it any baby
can transport you home?

– Ansie Baird

Contributors

Gay Baines (East Aurora, NY) is co-founder of July Literary Press, and is a member of the Roycroft Wordsmiths. Her novel, *Dear M.K.* (2002) was awarded Honorable Mention (Romance Category) in the review sponsored by the High Country Friends of the Toulumne County Library, Mi Wuk, CA. Her poems have appeared in *RE:AL, Rattapallax, ELF: Eclectic Literary Forum, The Baltimore Review, South Carolina Review, The Buffalo News, Storms* (July Literary Press, 2001) and many other publications.

Ansie Baird (Buffalo, NY) is Poet in Residence at The Buffalo Seminary. She has taught for Just Buffalo Literary Center in their Writers in Education program for the past twenty years. Her work has been published in *The Paris Review, Western Humanities Review, The Southern Review, The Denver Quarterly, Poetry Northwest,* and a number of other journals.

Walter Bargen (Ashland, MO) has recently published *The Feast* (BkMk Press-UMKC, 2004), and *The Body of Water* (Timberlake Press, 2003), among other books of poems. His work has appeared in *Iowa Review, New Letters, River City, Seattle Review, and Blue Mesa Review.*

Guy R. Beining (Lee, MA) has had more than 30 books and chapbooks of poetry and collage work published. His work has appeared recently in *Fence, Phoebe, The Portland Review, Bombay Gin, Ur Vox,* and *The New Orleans Review.*

Rema Boscov (Leverett, MA) is a poet, visual artist, and teacher, passionate about the natural world and our environment. She has been an artist-in-residence for two U.S. National Parks.

Patricia Brodie (Concord, MA) is a clinical social worker. Her poems have appeared, or are forthcoming, in *Poetry Motel, California Quarterly, Potpourri, Möbius, The Raintown Review,* and in anthologies. She recently won Honorable Mention in a New England Poetry Club contest.

Bill Brown (Greenbrier, TN) is the author of four collections of poems. He has been a Scholar in Poetry at the Bread Loaf Writers Conference, a Fellow at the Virginia Center for the Creative Arts and twice the recipient of the Poetry Fellowship from the Tennessee Arts Commission.

Carol Carpenter (Livonia, MI) has published poems and stories in *Yankee, America, Indiana Review, Quarterly Review,* and *Carolina Quarterly.* She has received many awards, including the Richard Eberhart Prize for Poetry.

Pam Clements (Albany, NY), a native of Buffalo, teaches English literature at Siena College. Her poems have appeared in *Earth's Daughters, Rapport, Screed, The Buffalo News,* and *Bardsong.*

Sandra Cookson (Buffalo, NY) is Professor of English and Chair of the English Department at Canisius College. She teaches courses in literature, modern poetry, and creative writing.

Laura Crews (West Springfield, MA) graduated from the University of North Carolina. Three of her poems were published in *Coraddi,* the undergraduate literary magazine. Since graduation in 2002, she continues to write and revise past works.

Gordon Crock (Snyder, NY) is an English teacher at Amherst High School. He appreciates this opportunity to sing his small song.

Margaret P. Cunningham was born in Mobile, Alabama, where she lives with her husband, Tom. She has written two novels and numerous short stories.

J.P. Dancing Bear (San Jose, CA) has poems published or forthcoming in *Atlanta Review, Poetry East, National Poetry Review, North American Review,* and others. He is editor of the *American Poetry Journal* and host of "Out of Our Minds," a weekly poetry program on public radio station KKUP. His latest book of poems is *Billy Last Crow* (Turning Point, 2004). His poem, "Near Solstice," appeared in July Literary Press' anthology *A Christmas Collection* (2001).

Carl Dennis (Buffalo, NY) is the author of numerous books of poetry. Though retired from the English faculty at the State University of New York at Buffalo, he still teaches emerging poets. His book *Practical Gods* won the Pulitzer Prize for Poetry in 2002.

Mary Ann Eichelberger is co-founder of July Literary Press, the author of *Is Midlife Easier in a Mink Coat*, a book of nonfiction, and two novels, *An Unpublished Writer*, and *A Cloud Slipped Across the Moon*, which was chosen Best Novel (Romance Category) in the 2003 review sponsored by the High Country Friends of the Toulumne County Library, Mi Wuk, CA. Her poetry first appeared in Poetry on the Buses and Poetry in Libraries; and has been published in *Storms* (July Literary Press, 2001), *The Buffalo News*, *Z Miscellaneous*, *ELF: Eclectic Literary Forum*, and many other publications.

Claire T. Feild (Auburn, AL) is Writing Consultant in the College of Business, Auburn University. Her poems have been published in *Runes, Möbius, The Carolina Quarterly*, and *South Dakota Review*. Her first book of poetry, *Mississippi Delta Women in Prism* complements portions of her memoir published in Boston's *Full Circle: A Journal of Poetry and Prose*.

Sally A. Fiedler (Buffalo, NY) has lived in Buffalo for more than thirty years, been a teacher for more than forty, and has written poems for more than fifty. She has two sons, six step-children (courtesy of her late husband, Leslie), and a host of step-grand-children and great-grandchildren. Her other name is Eleanor Mooseheart.

Catherine Gentile has had work published or forthcoming in *The Hurricane Review, The Long Story* and *The Ledge*. She lives on an island off the coast of Maine.

John Gilgun (St. Joseph, MO) is the author of several books of poetry, including *In The Zone: The Moby Dick Poems of John Gilgun* (Pecan Grove Press, 2002); *Your Buddy Misses You* (Three Phase, 1995); and *The Dooley Poems* (Robin Price, 1991).

Jimmie Margaret Gilliam (Williamsville, NY) is professor emerita of Erie County Community College in Buffalo. She teaches writing, conducts workshops, and is a well-known poet, editor and writer.

Bill Glose (Poquoson, VA) grew up in an Air Force Family. His eyes disqualified him from becoming a fighter pilot like his father, so he joined the 82d Airborne instead, spending five years as a paratrooper. His father still can't understand why anyone would jump out of a perfectly good airplane.

Ann Goldsmith (Buffalo, NY) is the author of *No One Is the Same Again*, a prizewinning book of poems published in 1999 by *The Quarterly Review of Literature*. Her work has appeared in numerous journals and anthologies. In 2002 her poem, "If You Don't Mind My Asking" was published in *Margie: The American of Poetry* as a winner in the St. Louis, MO Poetry Center's annual best poem contest, judged by Louise Gluck.

Ruth Holzer (Herndon, VA) works as a translator. Her poems have appeared or are forthcoming in *Exit 13, Connecticut River Review and The Formalist,* among others.

Ava Hu (Brooklyn, NY) graduated from Sarah Lawrence College. Her poems have appeared in *Worcester Review, Spoon River Poetry Review, Liberty Hill Poetry Review,* and in *The Pagan's Muse,* an anthology. She is the 2002 recipient of the AMY Poetry Award.

Christina K. Hutchins is a Ph.D. candidate in Interdisciplinary Studies at the Graduate Theological Union in Berkeley, CA. She has worked as a biochemist, a Congregational (UCC) minister, and teaches part time. Her chapbook *Collecting Light* was published by Acacia Books in 1999; and her poems appear widely in journals and anthologies.

Lorraine Jeffery (Circleville, OH) has published poems, short stories and articles in *Good Old Days, Mature Years,* and other journals. She is currently Coordinator of Children's Services at the public library in Chillicothe, Ohio.

Pearl Karrer (Palo Alto, CA) is a former microbiologist who teaches piano, exhibits art in juried shows, and writes poetry. She is an editor for the *California Quarterly*, and has had poems published in *Slant, Visions-International, Whetstone,* and other journals.

Alexander Levering Kern is a Quaker poet living outside Boston. His work is appeared or is forthcoming in *Clark Street Review, Rive Gauche, Out of Line, Spare Change News,* and *Quaker Life.* He teaches at Andover Newton Theological School.

Joseph Scott Kierland (Prescott, AZ) is a graduate of the University of Connecticut and the Yale Drama School. He was a resident playwright at New York's Lincoln Center, Brandeis University, and the Los Angeles Actor's Theatre. His first novel, *Rundown the Wind,* was published by Aegina Press.

Gabor Kovacsi (Snyder, NY) has published poetry in *The Nation, Exquisite Corpse, The Buffalo News,* and other publications.

Mary Laufer (Forest Grove, OR) is a native of East Aurora, NY. Her poetry has been published in *Proposing on the Brooklyn Bridge* (Grayson Books, 2003) and *Hunger Enough, Living Spiritually in a Consumer Society* (Pudding House, 2004).

Gabrielle LeMay (New York, NY) received her MFA in poetry from Hunter College in 2001. Her chapbook, *Pandora's Barn,* won the 2004 Tennessee Chapbook Prize, and is available from Middle Tennessee State University as an insert in *Poems & Plays 11.*

Karen Lewis (East Amherst, NY) is currently Contributing Editor for *Traffic East Magazine,* and the author of many poems, stories and essays. Her work has appeared in *The Buffalo News, Poetry Motel, The Red River Review,* and *Along the Path,* among others.

Lyn Lifshin's most recent prizewinning book (Paterson Poetry Award) *Before It's Light,* was published in winter 1999-2000 by Black Sparrow Press, which also published *Cold Comfort* in 1997. A new collection, *There Were Days, So Persephone* is forthcoming from Red Hen Press. She lives in Vienna, VA.

Kandace Brill Lombart (Amherst, NY) teaches at the State University of New York at Buffalo. She is working on a collection of memoirs about her late husband, Christian Ghislain Lombart.

Janet McCann (College Station, TX) was a 1989 NEA Creative Writing Fellowship winner. Her poems have appeared in *Kansas Quarterly, Parnassus, Nimrod,* and *New York Quarterly.* Her most recent book is *Looking for Buddha in the Barbed Wire Garden.* Her poem, "Looking at the Christmas Photos" appeared in July Literary Press' anthology *A Christmas Collection* (2001).

Matthew Murrey (Urbana, IL) has published poems in *The Progressive* and other journals, and received an NEA Fellowship for Poetry in 1995. He is seeking a publisher for his first book manuscript. He is a high school librarian and peace activist.

Jeanne Norwin lives in Williamsville, NY but her heart is in Paris. She is a reading junkie. This is her first appearance in print.

Michael Onofrey grew up in Los Angeles, but now lives in Japan, where he teaches English as a Second Language. His stories have appeared in *Oyez Review, Japanophile, Nagoya Writes,* and elsewhere.

Kenneth Pobo (Folsom, PA) is the author of *Introductions*, a book of poetry from Pearl's Book'Em Press (2003). His chapbook, *Postcards From America*, can be read online. He likes to garden and to collect obscure 1960s records.

Clare Poth is co-founder of Bryant Street Studio in Buffalo, NY. She is an artist and art educator. The watercolor paintings she produced for July Literary Press' previous books, *Storms* and *A Christmas Collection*, have been widely admired.

Elisavietta Ritchie (Broomes Island, MD) writes both poetry and fiction. Her most recent book is *In Haste I Write You This Note* won the Washington Writers' Publishing House Fiction Competition in 2002. Her poems have appeared in *The New York Times, The Christian Science Monitor, Nimrod,* and *The New Republic.* Her poem "Chicago 1938" appeared in July Literary Press' anthology *A Christmas Collection* (2001).

Gary Earl Ross (Buffalo, NY) is a professor of writing at the University at Buffalo Educational Opportunity Center. His books include *The Wheel of Desire and Other Intimate Hauntings* (2000), *Shimmerville* (2002), and the children's tale *Dots* (2002).

Deborah Miller Rothschild (Houston, TX) has had work published in *Houston Chronicle, My Table, The London Examiner, We Used to be Wives, Suddenly,* and *Zygote in My Coffee.com.*

Lynn Veach Sadler (Sanford, NC) is a former college president. She has published widely in academics and is now a full-time creative writer (fiction, poetry, and drama).

V. Jane Schneeloch (Springfield, MA) is retired high school English teacher. She participates in a weekly workshop with Pat Schneider and leads a writing workshop of previously incarcerated women. She has previously been published in *Peregrine.*

James Sedwick (East Aurora, NY) has had poems published in *Blueline, Passages North, The Buffalo News,* and *Uncharted Lines: Poems from the Journal of the American Medical Association.* He works as a clinical mental health school counselor.

Irma Sheppard (Tucson, AZ) received the Martindale Literary Award in 2000 and the Pam Mayall PCC Poetry Award in 2002. Her short stories and poems have been published in *Sandscript, Love Street Lamp post, Oasis, Facets Magazine* and *Portrait.*

Dan Sicoli (Niagara Falls, NY) co-edits *Slipstream Magazine* (www.slipstreampress.org). Pudding House Publications recently released two of his chapbooks, *Pagan Supper and the allegories.* He has been twice nominated for the Pushcart Prize.

Maggie Lamond Simone (Baldwinsville, NY) is an award-winning columnist and freelance writer in Central New York.

Dan Sklar (South Hamilton, MA) teaches writing at Endicott College where he tries to get his students to write in a natural and spontaneous way. His work has recently appeared in *Square Lake*, *Rhino*, *bowwow*, and *Mad Poets Review*.

Dorothy Stone (Concord, MA), a retired teacher, is also a published poet and essayist, nominated for a 2002 Pushcart Prize. She has an MFA in theatre based on work at Boston University and Yale. Her poem "Ice Age" appeared in July Literary Press— anthology *A Christmas Collection* (2001).

Parker Towle (Franconia, NH) is a clinical neurologist, teaches at Dartmouth Medical School. He also teaches at the Frost Festival of Poetry in Franconia each summer. Published writings include three chapbooks and an anthology of poems, *Exquisite Reaction*.

Michael Tritto (Buffalo, NY) has been writing poetry for a long time. His work has been published in journals throughout the US and recently, with help from the Internet, has been read in England and Ireland and (soon) in India. His poem "Never No" appeared in July Literary Press' anthology *A Christmas Collection*.

Jeff Walt (Honolulu, HI) received a 2003 fellowship from the Djerassi Foundation and was nominated for a 2003 and 2004 Pushcart Prize. His poetry has appeared or is forthcoming in *The Comstock Review*, *Harpur Palate*, *Hawai'i Review*.

Claudia Montague Wheatley (Newfield, NY), is a writer and editor for Communication and Marketing Service at Cornell University. Her essay "Take the Cruel Out of Yule" appeared in July Literary Press' anthology *A Christmas Collection* (2001).

Theresa Wyatt (Derby, NY) has been teaching for over 23 years, specializing in the student at risk. Formerly a practicing visual artist, she has recently returned to writing as an outlet for creative self-expression.

Natalia Zaretsky (Wharton, NJ) was born in Moscow, where she taught college physics. She emigrated to the US in 1983. Now retired, she writes poetry. Her first book of poetry, *Autumn Solstice* was published by Windsong RBC Publishing Company.

Andrena Zawinski (Oakland, CA) has been published in *Gulf Coast, Quarterly West, Rattle, Slipstream,* and other publications. Her full collection, *Traveling in Reflected Light,* was a Kenneth Patchen winner from Pig Iron Press; her latest chapbook is from Pudding House's Greatest Hits archival series. She is Features Editor at www.poetrymagazine.com .